"Jim?" McCoy Called . . .

"No point in going in there. They're both out cold."

Kirk stopped at the entrance to the little room and half-turned his head toward the doctor. McCoy could not see his face. "Just wanted to check on Anitra," he said easily. "No harm in that, is there?"

There was a heartbeat's pause. No harm, that McCoy could see . . . yet there was something wrong with the question, with the way that Kirk stood in the doorway. McCoy realized that the hairs on his scalp and neck were standing straight up.

"Dear God," McCoy whispered. "Jim—"

Kirk's back relaxed. "Something wrong, Doctor?"

"Yes. Yes, there's something wrong," McCoy croaked, forcing the words from his throat against their will. In the midst of his terror, he was suddenly struck by anger at what had been done to his friend. "Just what in hell *are* you?"

Look for STAR TREK Fiction from Pocket Books

DEMONS

J.M. DILLARD

A STAR TREK® NOVEL

POCKET BOOKS

New York   London   Toronto   Sydney   Tokyo

Another *Original* publication of POCKET BOOKS

POCKET BOOKS, a division of Simon & Schuster Inc.
1230 Avenue of the Americas, New York, N.Y. 10020

ISBN: 0-671-66150-7

First Pocket Books printing July 1986

10 9 8 7 6 5

POCKET and colophon are trademarks of
Simon & Schuster Inc.

Printed in the U.S.A.

PROLOGUE

Beekman's Planet. Its nearness to binary suns and oppressive humidity made it hot, even for Vulcans, but unlike home, Beekman's was lush and wet. Up in the mountains it was cooler, and atop the smallest of them, T'Ylle sat on her heels, shading her eyes from the glare. It had been said that she was beautiful, and that her eyes made her so: they were large and almond-shaped, with an upward slant, as velvety blue-black as her hair. To T'Ylle, the fact had never been of the least importance: there was a remoteness about them as well that was impenetrable.

T'Ylle pulled back the hood of her jacket and brushed the moisture from the face of the tricorder. The afternoon rains had just ended, and the leaves, coated with tiny droplets, made the glade glisten like a jewel. Steam rose from the ground around her boots with a soft hiss. She scanned the area briefly, and the results pleased her—she was the only animal life form in the immediate vicinity. Danger was, at least for the moment, averted. She let the tricorder dangle again from the strap on her shoulder and peered over the precipice.

Below, tiny workers crawled out from under make-shift shelters and began digging in the heavy muck, made heavier still by the fresh rain. In spite of the limitations imposed by the climate and soil conditions, work on the dig had progressed beyond their expectations. They had originally anticipated at least another year, but it was rumored that Starnn would declare their decades of work finished sometime within the next few days. Already they were close to exhausting this site—the last—of its treasure. *And do they know,* thought T'Ylle, *what they have unearthed?*

Save for those already affected, none of the others suspected. . . .

Perhaps it was foolish of her to confront the danger this boldly, but family relationships demanded no less. She could not go to the others, not until she had confirmation from his own lips first. If not foolish, then she was at the very least reckless . . . but the chance existed that she could set things aright, or that she had been wrong, had entirely misunderstood.

But she knew she had not.

She repressed, so much from habit that she was no longer aware of it and would have denied it, a shudder at the thought of what would happen if she were killed. The gesture had arisen not from fear of her own mortality, but of what would follow for the others—not only the expedition, but the billions back home. . . .

She rose expectantly at the sound of steps crushing the low, sun-baked undergrowth, but did not use the tricorder to tell her what approached. At present only one species of animal life on the planet was capable of such footfall. The footsteps shuffled and came to a halt.

At the same time, something buzzed loudly past her, grazing her face. Disconcerted, she stepped back and raised the tricorder in front of her face as protection. When the assailant flew past again, she struck out at it. The insect fell on its back in the soil, its legs dancing maniacally in the air. Without hesitation, T'Ylle lowered her foot over it and with a quick, firm movement, crushed it. Her mouth twitched slightly as the hard shell made a loud crunch beneath her boot.

The visitor stood silently and watched the murder without reaction; T'Ylle raised serene, fearless eyes to meet his.

"You see," she said, "I know everything."

Chapter One

THE BUILDING, WHICH housed the sister sciences of linguistics, anthropology, and archaeology, was more than three thousand years old, but it could scarcely be distinguished from the younger buildings on the campus of the Vulcan Science Academy. The structure's design was a wonder of the architecture of the period—naturally lit by the sun and ventilated by captured desert breezes, it had taken no notice of the passage of three millennia, save for the addition of artificial nighttime lighting and computer equipment in the labs. Outside, the hot wind rippled red sand into tiny dunes under a blinding sun; inside, it was fresh and cool and dim.

The ceilings in the ancient building were high, and the heels of Sarek's boots echoed loudly on the stone stairs. He climbed until he reached the third floor (he would not have used the lift even if there had been one) and walked to the end of the hallway, to the door bearing the inscription LINGUISTICS. He paused before the door and spoke a name aloud—the offices were not equipped with buzzers—and waited for a response too soft for human ears before he pushed against the heavy stone door.

In the center of the room was a desk and behind it a

window flooded the room with sunlight, obscuring for a moment the face of the seated figure in shadow. Sarek blinked. The figure rose and stepped forward out of the glare.

Silek was younger, leaner, with an openness about him that Sarek completely lacked, but even so the resemblance was unmistakable. He raised his hand in the Vulcan salute. "It has been many years, brother."

Sarek returned the salute. "Many years; thirty-eight point four standard, to be exact."

"I trust your wife and son are well?"

"They are well." Sarek paused politely, taking notice of the stranger who stood next to Silek's desk.

Silek turned to him deferentially. "This is Starnn, my father-in-law. Starnn was chief archaeologist on our project. He will be participating in the presentation with us."

"Sarek," Sarek addressed the old Vulcan. "Then you are part of our family, and will be staying with us."

Out of respect for Starnn's age, which he estimated to be well over two hundred, Sarek waited for the older man to initiate the salute. But Starnn merely nodded distractedly. His white hair was disheveled, as though he had forgotten to comb it, and there was a vacant gaze in his eyes. Sarek took no offense; even the best of Vulcans sometimes suffered from forgetfulness at such advanced age.

"Starnn, of course, has often heard me mention your name, and is honored," Silek said swiftly.

Sarek changed the subject. "And what of your expedition to the Hydrilla sector?"

"Most successful, actually," replied Silek. "Of the

ruins, we were only able to thoroughly explore Beekman's Planet, which is why we need more funding to continue exploration of the sector."

"If you were successful, no doubt you uncovered some interesting artifacts," Sarek said, looking at Starnn.

"Of course," Starnn said in a wavering voice, suddenly galvanized. "That is why we must return. There were far too many for us to uncover in one expedition. And several of these discoveries are worthy of extensive study and testing, for they will no doubt lead to a greater understanding of the principles of physics." He turned to Silek. "Show him the box."

"Yes," said Silek. "One of our most intriguing discoveries." He went into the lab for a moment, then returned to the outer office area with a look of thinly veiled scientific excitement and what looked to be a smooth piece of onyx, polished so that its surface reflected the faces of the three. It was somewhat larger than Silek's hand, and shaped like a Terran oyster, with an almost invisible seam around its center. Even in the daylight, a faint bluish glow emanated from it. Sarek thought he detected a slight hum.

"Try to open it." Silek handed it to him.

Sarek pulled on the top of the box and flinched as it sparked and crackled. "I cannot."

"Nor can we," replied Silek, "with all of our instruments. It is apparently an internally generated force field. And it is shielded from us; our scanners cannot penetrate this material. We don't even know if the structure is solid or hollow. And, of course, the field will not permit us to analyze the material."

"Fascinating," said Sarek.

"And quite beautiful," said Starnn. "An ingenious blending of the principles of physics and art to create a puzzle. We found many others like it; this one is the smallest. Please take it as a gift, a souvenir of the Hydrilla sector."

Silek shot a quizzical glance at the elderly Vulcan.

"Forgive me," said Sarek, "but I cannot take it. This belongs to the academy museum. It belongs where others can appreciate it."

Starnn ignored Silek's stern, silent gaze. "We already have too many for display. This one is the smallest, as I said."

"I cannot," said Sarek.

Starnn grew something close to vehement. "You are a diplomat," he said. "Your house is open to many guests, some of them interplanetary; the box would be seen and enjoyed by many."

"Perhaps you are right." Sarek bowed slightly, wishing at this point only to humor him. "I am honored."

"Your acceptance honors me," Starnn said, mollified.

"If you gentlemen are ready," Sarek said, "I will escort you to my home."

"Yes," Silek agreed quickly. "And will your family be there also?"

"My wife will be there. Spock is in Star Fleet."

"Forgive me," said Starnn. "I have some matters to attend to here in the capital. If it is no inconvenience, I will join you later."

"Certainly," said Sarek. "Take the evening shuttle to ShiKahr and I will meet you at the station."

Starnn nodded and picked up the box. "Do not

forget this. I know you will display it where it can be admired.''

Sarek bowed again as he accepted the box.

The two left. In the hallway, out of Starnn's earshot, Sarek said, "I am honored by the gift, but I feel it is inappropriate. I am unused to receiving items which should be museum pieces."

"Starnn uncovered many of these," Silek answered, not meeting his brother's eyes. "He is quite accurate when he says that there are too many for display."

"Then it could be used for testing. And I perceive that you also do not approve of Starnn's action."

Silek paused before he met Sarek's eyes. "Starnn may be chief archaeologist, but even that does not give him the right to dispose of academy property."

"Then why did you say nothing to him?"

"He has not been himself of late."

"He is old," said Sarek. "And his only daughter has died."

Silek glanced at him darkly. "My wife. Yet I have not changed. It's more than that. Even before T'Ylle died, Starnn . . . changed."

"Perhaps he should visit a healer."

"If you could recommend a local one," Silek said, "I will suggest it to him."

"That would be wise," said Sarek.

Silek paused, and his tone became lighter. "And is the lady Amanda still as gracious as I remember her?"

Sarek was unaware that his expression had softened. "Even more so."

A diamond-eyed beetle with mother-of-pearl wings droned in through the open window of the archaeology dating laboratory. Starnn took no notice; his eyes were focused on a row of silvery onyx boxes all weakly glowing in the daylit room. He did not see the insect until it had the misfortune of lighting on one of the luminous boxes. Starnn cupped his hands and gently caught the creature, moving toward the open window to free it; but a spasm shook him before he was able to unclasp his hands. It passed swiftly, leaving his face locked in a hideous grimace. The grimace resolved itself into a serene smile as he set the beetle carefully upon the windowsill, and with long, bony fingers, proceeded to pull off its delicate, iridescent wings.

"I just don't understand, sir," Lisa Nguyen said. "Why are we picking up only a handful of the expedition?"

The security contingent of Tomson, Nguyen and al-Baslama had seen to it that the Vulcan researchers were safely ensconced in their quarters and were now making their way back to C deck. Nguyen was the newest member of the security team, and the lowest in rank. She had directed this question deferentially to Security Chief Tomson.

Tomson gave Nguyen a sideways glance, secretly displeased, although technically she had no right to be. Nguyen was eager and well-scrubbed enough, with hair pulled back and falling in an amazingly straight line down her back. It was the hair that troubled Tomson; she could not get used to the new, relaxed regulations on hairstyle. Tomson was regular navy, and still had palpitations when a crewman's hair touched the collar. She made a mental note to talk to Nguyen afterwards. For routine security work, okay—but for show, pomp and circumstance, the hair should be pinned up. Nguyen might not like it, of course; if she decided to be bold, she could point out to Tomson that this was a backwater planet in a dead sector and the Vulcans they were picking up were scientists, not diplomats. . . . She could point it out, and find herself transferred. Tomson was not there to be liked. She was there to see to it that her people did their job.

Nguyen smiled up uncertainly at her, and Tomson's pale face shifted into the barest ghost of a smile. It was often an effort for her to be friendly, especially with overeager types like Nguyen. She'd once overheard a crewman saying that it must be the altitude—it wasn't the first such comment she'd heard. A cold, six-and-a-half-foot female security chief was an easy target for jokes. Tomson told herself she did not care, as long as it didn't interfere with her job.

"They were staying behind to finish up an archaeological dig, and one of them was injured," Tomson answered, looking straight ahead and not at Nguyen. "All of their doctors had already left, and he needed immediate medical attention. The *Enterprise* was the closest ship out. Apparently, his family came with him."

"Extended family," al-Baslama said. He was swarthy, congenial, and almost as tall as Tomson. Save for his intelligence, he perfectly fit the stereotype of the beefy security guard.

Nguyen nodded; they had picked up twelve passengers. "Do they always travel in families like that?"

"It was convenient in this instance," Tomson said. "They'd been out close to forty years."

"Forty years . . ." Nguyen faltered.

Tomson shrugged. "The wink of an eye, to a Vulcan." She stopped abruptly as they approached the turbolift and turned to al-Baslama. "I wonder if I could talk to you for a minute, al-B."

"Of course, sir."

Nguyen got on the turbolift and shot a glance in al-Baslama's direction, which he studiously ignored. From the looks of things, Nguyen had already joined the ranks of al-B's ardent admirers; no doubt, she had hoped to ditch Tomson and consult al-B about his off-duty plans. Tomson watched the doors close over her with a sense of smugness.

Al-Baslama stood politely at attention, and Tomson looked at him admiringly. Next to Tomson, he held the highest rank of anyone else in security: lieutenant, junior grade. Not, Tomson thought, that he hadn't earned it. Now that Nguyen was gone, she permitted herself to smile at him. Al-B relaxed; he had not been able to tell from the lieutenant's voice whether to expect praise or a reprimand.

Tomson never wasted words. "I've recommended you be put up for promotion. I want you to know that my evaluation of you was extremely flattering."

"Sir?" al-Baslama said. He wasn't due for a promotion for another six months. He was silent for a moment and then seemed to remember that more of a response was called for. "Thank you, sir. That's very kind."

Tomson leaned forward conspiratorially and lowered her voice. "I'll tell you another secret, al-B. I'm almost sure you're going to get it."

He hesitated. "Sir . . . that would mean a transfer."

"I suppose it would," Tomson said, falsely casual. It was not something she liked to think about, but someone like al-B deserved any help he got from his superiors. "You deserve a command of your own. We both know that."

"But I've enjoyed working with you, sir," al-B protested. "You're the best."

Tomson lowered her eyes, uncharacteristically embarrassed. "I appreciate the compliment, Lieutenant, but you've got a career to think of. You shouldn't let anything get in its way."

"Yes, sir," he said, clearly unconvinced. "Again, thank you, sir."

Tomson stepped into the turbolift, and al-B followed. He stood, silent, not looking at her, as they moved toward C deck.

When she could no longer stand the silence, she said, slightly exasperated, "Is there a problem, Lieutenant?"

Al-B squared his shoulders. "Is there any way, sir, that I could get the promotion and still be assigned to the *Enterprise?*"

Nguyen, Tomson thought bitterly. She almost stamped her foot. "Dammit, al-B, I stuck my neck out on this one! What's the matter with you? There's no one on this ship worth wasting your career for!"

"I had thought . . ." he said softly, then broke off. "I guess I was wrong."

Tomson was about to continue her invective until she caught his eye. She had only seen such looks directed at others, never at herself—and she became

17

suddenly conscious of her heart beating faster. "Moh . . ." she said gently. "I'm your immediate superior. It wouldn't be proper."

"I know, sir. But a transfer . . ." He looked hard at her. "I guess I read everything wrong. Is that what you really want?"

"Yes—for your career," Tomson insisted. Then, in a much lower voice, she said, "Personally? No. You're the best person, male or female, I've ever had on this team . . . and the nicest."

He smiled sadly. "Maybe it won't go through, Lieutenant."

The doors to the turbolift opened. "Don't be a damn fool," she said shortly, and walked away too quickly for him to catch up.

Amanda had finished planting and was just watering the last rosebush when Sarek brought Silek back into the garden. She straightened suddenly, smiled, and then grimaced.

"Are reunions always painful for you, my wife?" Sarek asked calmly.

"It's nothing," she said, smiling once again. "A thorn. Silek, how wonderful to see you!" Her impulse was to hold out her hand in the Vulcan embrace, two fingers extended, but a strange shyness held her back. "You've hardly changed."

It was true, of course; other than a broad streak of gray in the front of his hair, Silek looked exactly the same. Being human and aging much faster, Amanda knew that he could not truthfully say the same for her; after living with a Vulcan for many years, she did not expect him to. Curious, though, how much he looked like Spock. . . . She had never forgotten his face, but had somehow failed to realize over the years that by some capricious combination of genes, her son had grown to look more like his uncle than his own father.

"How long has it been?" she asked.

"Thirty-eight-point-four years, or so your husband tells me." Silek did not smile, but the effect was the same as if he had. Amanda wondered how he did it.

Sarek held out his hand to her in the ritual embrace; automatically, she walked over to the two men and touched her fingertips to her husband's. Sarek looked down at her hand and permitted himself the small, exasperated tug at one corner of his mouth that usually appeared only when he teased her in private. "Your hands are dirty, my wife. I see that you have forgotten your gloves again."

"I'm not afraid of a little dirt," Amanda replied, pretending defiance, but she wiped her hands again on her coveralls. "Ouch!"

"The thorn?" Sarek asked. "Let me see."

Amanda held up her thumb and did not flinch as Sarek removed the thorn with expert detachment. "So you see," Sarek said under his breath to Silek, "what marrying an Earther has brought me." A small rill of blood followed the thorn, and she instinctively pulled her dirty thumb away from Sarek and put it in her mouth.

"Barbaric." Silek turned to Sarek. "Is it typical to find her thus—covered with dirt?"

Sarek nodded. "She has always been fond of gardening; indeed, she knows more now about Vulcan gardening than I. But it has always been her private sorrow that roses could not survive the climate here.

19

She tells me now that a genus of rose has been developed which can withstand life on Vulcan."

"For her sake, I hope it survives," said Silek, remembering that roses had always been her favorite flower.

Amanda smiled. "This time I am determined. Neither hot Vulcan breezes nor infernal pests are going to destroy my flowers this time. But here, let me clean up." She brushed the dark, loamy soil from her coveralls. "I wasn't expecting you back so soon; this isn't exactly my hostess gown."

"Finish your gardening," Silek said. "If we were on Earth, I'd say I am family, not company. And it is quite nice in the garden."

"On Vulcan the best kind of company is family," Amanda retorted. "Besides, I'm finished. I'll be only a few minutes." She turned and went into the house.

"I have never seen such black soil," said Silek.

"Earth dirt," Sarek replied. "For Earth flowers. Imported all the way from Minnesota, knowing my wife."

Silek walked carefully through the fresh mounds of earth and leaned over the nearest bush to inspect it. There were no buds. "These would be yellow roses," he said suddenly.

Sarek studied him curiously. "I was unaware you were such a horticulture expert, Silek. These are a yellow variety known as Desert Peace."

Silek straightened. "I cannot claim such expertise, Sarek, merely a simple deduction. I was recalling a conversation when Amanda mentioned her favorite flower."

"You have an excellent memory, brother."

*   *   *

Thirty-nine years ago, Georgetown. It was Silek's first protracted stay on Terra, and the weather there had been abominable—freezing cold in the winter, cool but humid in the summer. It was Amanda who made it all infinitely more tolerable. As an exchange student in the doctoral program, he taught linguistics to undergraduates; Amanda, in the same program, shared the office with him.

There was something of the rebel in Silek. The fact that he was at Georgetown attested to it: he had gone despite his father's savage protests. It was a matter of personal pride for him; he had explained patiently to his father that he had no interest in politics and diplomacy, and that his talents lay elsewhere. But Skon would not hear of any divergence from the family tradition; Silek would attend the academy, as his elder brother had, and would follow in the path of his father, and his father's father. . . .

Silek chose instead to be *ktorr skann*, without a family. It had not been an easy decision—the formal cutting of ties, forbidding him ever to return to the house of his father—but it was the only one he could have made. It was no small irony to Silek that following his own path led him to Washington, where his ultra-conformist brother worked at the embassy. The relationship between the two was not without its strains; although Silek told himself he was incapable of feelings of jealousy or competition, he experienced them nonetheless. And anger, perhaps, at his brother, for always doing the correct thing, for never questioning the old ways. After the formal declaration of Silek's apostasy from the family, he doubted whether Sarek would even acknowledge his presence there:

Sarek, pride of his father, pride of the entire family, no doubt soon to be appointed ambassador to Terra. Silek was quite shocked when Sarek risked their father's wrath by receiving his younger brother with his usual reserve. Perhaps Sarek was changing; perhaps he, too, was learning to question.

Amanda made Silek question himself more than any other being he had known. Many times he had asked himself what it was about her, what it could possibly be, that made her so unlike any other female he had met.

Yet it was he who had introduced her to Sarek after hearing of the need for an English tutor who was willing to teach at the embassy. Because of Silek's glowing recommendations, Sarek interviewed her himself. And out of family loyalty, it was Silek who convinced her to marry Sarek, after he had already realized the extent of her feelings for his brother and had condemned himself to forget his own.

Thirty-nine years ago, Silek walked into his small, windowless office and found Amanda sitting, looking at the cascade of roses which covered her desk. He had asked her the significance of the flowers.

"I wish I knew," she said and looked up at last with her clear blue eyes. "I wonder if the person who sent them knows."

"Sarek." He stated it flatly, like a fact. "What do you mean, if he knows?"

Amanda looked down at her desk again and didn't speak for a moment. Silek went over to the door and closed it softly behind him.

"Red roses signify love," she said, still not looking at him. "I'm sure that he doesn't realize that. I think he's just following what he thinks is a polite custom. He knows I'm fond of roses."

"He is, at least, attempting to please you." Silek's desk was perpendicular to hers; he turned his chair sideways to face her. "Isn't that significant?"

Amanda didn't seem to hear the question; she looked up at him with a sudden intensity. "Do you know of any marriages between Vulcans and humans, Silek?"

The question caught him off guard. "No . . . I have not been informed of any. However, I wouldn't be surprised—"

"Not surprised?" Amanda seemed to be. "Most people would be shocked at the idea."

"Only those who have not met you, Amanda." Silek leaned back in his chair, not quite able to believe that he had actually said it.

She was too agitated to understand what he was saying. "I need your help, Silek. I need to be . . . logical about this. . . ."

Is it logic you want, Amanda, he thought; but he said, "You are in love with Sarek?"

Amanda nodded, miserable. "But I mustn't expect anything in return from him. I know how pathetically emotional I must appear. . . . But if you could just explain it to me—if you could tell me what his motives are—I can't understand them."

"Sarek doesn't tell you how he feels," Silek said quietly. Again, it was a statement of fact, not a question.

"Yes."

Silek almost smiled, then turned his face away and spoke in a voice that Amanda found almost inaudible. "How you underestimate yourself, my lady." He looked back at her. "You are aware, of course, of the origin of your own name?"

"I hadn't thought about it." Amanda, the linguist, was embarrassed.

"Old Earth Latin. It means 'lovable.' Your parents named you well."

Silek watched with interest as Amanda's face flushed red, but she continued to struggle toward her objective. "Do you think—is it possible—Sarek loves me?"

"Roses do not symbolize logic, Amanda. And I know my brother is well versed in any human custom he practices. He is, after all, chief aide to the Terran ambassador."

Amanda raised a hand to her red cheek and looked at her roses.

Silek continued. "But he cannot be pressed to use the same words and gestures you use, Amanda. Let his actions express his feelings; we Vulcans are unaccustomed to the use of words when it comes to such matters."

"I think he is going to ask me to marry him," she said with great effort. "And I don't know what to say, because I didn't know if he could care for me."

"At the risk of betraying my race, the Vulcan who says he has no feelings is a liar. We are trained to suppress them, Amanda. We are not born without them. But you must not expect Sarek to suddenly act like a human male in love."

"No," she said. "Then he wouldn't be Sarek. But I worry that the family wouldn't accept me . . . and I worry what would happen if we had children. . . ."

"The family will accept what Sarek tells them to accept," Silek said, not without some irony. "And as for children . . . what two better parents can you think of?"

Amanda smiled at him, suddenly radiant. "Silek, thank you. If I could hug you, I would."

Silek straightened nervously in his chair. "That would be . . . inappropriate. Here. You'll need to know this soon enough anyway." He stretched out his hand, two fingers extended, toward her. "For family," he said. "Welcome."

Smiling, she touched her fingers to his.

Awkwardly, he joked, "Of course, you needn't tell Sarek where you learned this."

Amanda laughed and turned back to her desk. "Red roses," she said, her voice rising giddily, though she fought to keep it level. "Actually, yellow are my favorite, but I'm glad he didn't send any."

"Is the color significant?"

"Yellow roses are for parting. Good-byes."

"Interesting," Silek said noncommittally.

The day he returned to Vulcan, Amanda found a single yellow rose on her desk.

Skon died soon after, and Silek's mother received her youngest son back into the family, as was her right. Soon afterward, Silek's marriage to another member of the expedition was arranged shortly before he and his bride left for Hydrilla. So it was that Sarek, the conformist, took a human wife, while his outcast brother returned to Vulcan for the traditional bonding.

They sat in the large central room before dinner—Silek in Sarek's favorite chair, Amanda on the sofa. Sarek had gone to retrieve Starnn from the shuttle station. Silek was studying the portrait of mother and son that hung above the piano.

"A very good likeness of you," Silek said. "How old was your son when this was painted?"

"Ten," said Amanda. "It's a good likeness of him, too."

"I look forward to meeting my nephew someday. You say that he is in Star Fleet?"

Amanda nodded. "He's a commander on a starship."

"Commander. Then he has risen to a high rank in a very short time. No doubt he will soon be a captain." Silek paused. "I must admit that I am . . . somewhat impressed at Sarek's acceptance of his son's choice of career. Vulcan fathers are not always tolerant of deviations from the family pattern."

"Spock and his father have reached an understanding. I won't say that it was easy." She smiled at him. "But you haven't spoken at all about your expedition to the Hydrilla sector. And I'm very interested in hearing about your experience as a linguist in the field."

Silek lifted one eyebrow a millimeter to indicate that he understood her reason for changing the subject and respected her loyalty toward Sarek. "The number of documents I was able to unearth and translate was staggering, but most of the work is behind me. Except—"

"Except?" asked Amanda.

"The brief inscription that appears on the unusual boxes we found. As a matter of fact, your husband has one of the boxes here. The opinion of another linguist is always helpful."

Silek disappeared for a few moments and returned with two items. He held one of them out to Amanda. "I forgot to give this to you earlier."

"What is this?" she asked with delight and opened the book. "Copyright nineteen thirty-eight . . . 'The Creator sat upon the throne, thinking . . .' " She smiled up at him. "Silek, thank you, this is wonderful! Where did you manage to find this?"

"In the capital. You don't have it, do you?" he asked. "I have always remembered your fondness for them. . . . I saw you had amassed quite a collection."

"I don't have it. And I love Twain. Thank you very much." She closed the book lovingly and set it next to her on the couch. Silek ignored the thanks and held the next item out to Amanda, who hesitated as though she were afraid to touch it. "What is it?" she asked.

"My associate Starnn would tell you it's a work of art. I'm not so certain. It is, however, shielded against scanners and protected against opening by a force field. We found several others like this one." He turned it over so that Amanda could see the inscription etched into the smooth surface.

Amanda ran her fingers over it and shook her head. "I couldn't even begin to guess its origin. There are no familiar points of references, no similarities to anything I've ever seen." She looked up at him. "Have you considered that it might simply be a meaningless decoration?"

"Yes. But the computer indicates that if it were simply a decorative pattern, it would repeat its design more often. It has the mixture of redundancy and novelty one expects to find in language. But it's quite unlike any of the languages in the Hydrilla sector. I'm most familiar with the Beekmanian languages, of course, and it's certainly not like any of those. One of my theories is that it's an ancient script of some proto-Beekmanian language lost in some earlier global catastrophe—a form of script which died out. My problem has been that there's too small a sample of it for the computer to break the code."

"And how long ago did that civilization die out?"

" 'Die out' is a misleading term. Roughly one thousand solar years ago, the civilization destroyed itself."

"War?" Amanda asked.

"Perhaps you could call it that. In most cases, the population seems to have brutally murdered each other. A plague of some type, probably. Whatever happened, the destruction was sudden . . . and thorough. And not just Beekman's Planet. All inhabited planets in the sector were affected the same way, over a period of time."

"They must have been quite sophisticated to develop something like this," Amanda mused, looking at the box.

"Our excavations don't give us much clue as to how they managed it. Their technology was no more advanced than ours, yet we have nothing like this. My guess is that this was left behind during a visit from a more advanced civilization; but as to who that might be, we have no clue. All we know is that if such a visit took place, it was before the destruction. Starnn unearthed these himself and verifies that they had been buried for at least one thousand years. Therefore, it is unlikely that the visit had anything to do with the destruction of the planet."

"Maybe they opened the box," Amanda joked.

Tomson was in the rec lounge drinking a solitary Scotch when al-Baslama entered.

"Mind if I join you?" he asked. His expression was unusually serious.

Tomson nodded at the chair next to her. Al-B sat in it.

"I got that promotion," he said. "I want you to know I appreciate everything you've done."

She forced a smile. "Moh, that's great! Congratulations!"

"Thank you," he said expressionlessly.

She quit smiling and frowned slightly. "You don't look too happy about it, Lieutenant. I think we'd better do something about that. I've got just the thing." She went over to the bar and programmed up another Scotch. She brought it back and held it out to him. "To your promotion," she said, smiling again. He took it slowly. Tomson held up her glass encouragingly. "Cheers," she said.

Moh said nothing, but drank his Scotch, keeping his eyes on her the whole time. When they put their glasses down, he said, "I report to the *Valor* as the new security chief."

In spite of herself, she said quickly, "When?"

"A week from yesterday."

Tomson silently repeated this to herself. "That's great! I'm really happy for you." She should be happy, she told herself, but still she felt a sinking feeling in the pit of her stomach. "The *Valor*'s a good ship. Chen Szu-Yi's an excellent captain."

Moh nodded. "Of course, the promotion is effective immediately. I'm a full lieutenant as of today."

"Full lieutenant," Tomson said and swallowed her Scotch. "Well, since we're equals, I suppose you can call me Ingrit."

"Ingrit," he said awkwardly. "I wonder, Ingrit . . ."

Tomson looked at him expectantly.

"We're equals now." Moh leaned forward across the table. "Does this . . . change things?"

He was leaving in a week. Tomson threw her head back and finished her Scotch. "I suppose it does," she said, meeting his eyes fearlessly.

They left the lounge together.

Sarek awoke with a gasp. He was in his bedroom, in the darkness, lying next to his wife. He looked over at her to see if he had disturbed her, but she lay on her side, breathing in soft, regular sighs.

He sat up in the bed and, with a great effort of will, ceased trembling. He had had a dream—no, he had had a nightmare, an experience quite alien to him. On a few occasions he had listened tolerantly, almost smugly, to his wife as she recounted her own bad dreams, and he had knowingly reassured her of their insignificance. Vulcans dreamed, of course—most sapient creatures do—but Sarek's were dreams of everyday occurrences, reflections of reality, the brain playing back the day's events to index what was important in the memory and dispose of the rest. He had never before understood the depth of terror such outwardly simple, even ridiculous images could evoke in the night.

He closed his eyes and remembered. Jeweled insects—thousands of them, flying and crawling. But something was amiss; the insects fell from the air, their wings torn and missing, limbs pulled off, shells crushed. They lay on their backs and waved their remaining legs in the air in agony. The image was still capable of evoking horror in him, but at the same time made absolutely no sense. He had encountered no such insects nor had he seen anything mutilated recently. Yet the dream disturbed him to the point that he found it impossible to return to sleep.

He sat for a moment on the bed, listening to Amanda's breathing until it became absolutely clear to him that he could no longer remain in bed. He would go to his study and read. The idea made perfect sense, but something in him quite illogically resisted. The notion persisted until at last he rose, dressed himself and went into the central room. In the darkness he imagined that he could see a faint blue glow emanating from his study; but when he entered, he saw that the box was not glowing. The force field had been lowered.

"Fascinating," he said and bent down to open the box.

In the bedroom, Amanda cried out softly in her sleep.

Chapter Two

IT WAS CROWDED in the rec lounge, as was usual for the time of day: early evening, for those just coming off the first shift. Kirk had joined the small group watching Spock and his opponent and had just caught a glimpse of Tomson and al-Baslama surreptitiously gliding out when McCoy wandered in with a bottle of beer in his hand.

"What's the matter, Bones?" Kirk asked. "Did the distillery finally run dry?"

"God forbid," McCoy said fervently. "Can't a man do things a little differently once in a while?"

"No law against it. But forgive me if I stick with my usual." Kirk took another sip of his brandy.

"No law against that stuff—but there ought to be." McCoy sat down and took a long pull on his bottle. "Well, I'll be damned. Looks like Spock has a new protégée. When did she come on board?"

Kirk smiled tiredly. "Nearly a week ago. You haven't been paying attention much lately, have you?"

"I guess not," McCoy said, staring quite openly at the woman who sat across the chessboard from Spock.

32

The most striking thing about her was most likely her hair: flame red, thick and waving down her back, a startling contrast to her white complexion. Her expression was far less exuberant than her hair. She leaned forward, elbows on the board, resting a very sharp chin on one fist, and the look on her face was a perfect reflection of Spock's. Were it not for the ears and that hair, McCoy thought, you'd think she was a Vulcan.

"Care to make a little wager? Two to one says Spock wins."

"What kind of odds are those?" McCoy complained. "Of course, he's gonna win. But you can put me down for five credits just on principle in favor of the young lady."

Kirk shrugged. "It's not that sure of a bet, Bones. That young lady is Dr. Anitra Lanter."

McCoy groaned. *"Doctor?* I *am* getting old. She can't be more than twenty years old."

"Twenty-four," Kirk said.

"Twenty-four," McCoy sighed and shook his head. "Twenty-four. I was twenty-four once."

"You? You were never twenty-four."

"Ah . . ." McCoy turned his attention to his beer.

"So the name Lanter means nothing to you?"

"Should it?"

"Hermann Lanter, the famous physicist?"

"Oh, yeah," McCoy said without enthusiasm. "Wasn't he a genius or something?"

"Or something," Kirk said. "And that's his daughter."

"Well, dammit, Jim, why didn't you tell me sooner?

I'd have put *ten* credits on her." McCoy belched softly.

"What? And be out twenty credits?" Kirk said, smiling, as the intercom whistled. He went over to it, and McCoy watched the captain's expression turn sourer with each passing second as he listened and argued by turns for a full minute.

"What is it?" McCoy asked when he returned. "You don't look too pleased, Jim."

"Orders for shore leave." Kirk sat down abruptly and nursed his drink, staring straight ahead at the chess game without really seeing it.

"Don't tell me. Canceled again."

"Not canceled—changed. Star Fleet figures that since we're dropping off the last of the Hydrillan researchers on Vulcan, we can just . . . take shore leave there."

"If that's supposed to be a joke, Jim, that's not very funny."

Kirk did not smile. "Komack's orders."

"But Star Base Five is close enough and would be a hell of a lot more fun. Why would they want to change our orders?"

"Ask Komack," Kirk said glumly.

"Komack's gone nuts," McCoy muttered into his beer. "Too bad I'm not chief medical officer for the fleet. I'd have him certified unfit for duty so fast. . . . Why would anyone in their right mind want to take leave on Vulcan?"

Kirk sighed. "I can think of at least one person on board this ship who would."

They watched in glum silence for a few more moments. It looked as though Spock would easily rout the young woman, until she looked up at him with a sudden, surprising impishness, stuck out her tongue, and moved her queen.

McCoy sat forward, suddenly brightening. "Check-mate. Well, I'll be . . . I think I'm in love. Hey, where're you going, Jim? You owe me ten credits."

Later that evening, McCoy stopped by sickbay to check in with M'Benga and very nearly collided with Anitra Lanter on the way out. She leaned against the door, tightlipped and breathing heavily, one arm gripping her midsection, the mischievous glimmer in her eyes replaced by something very close to dull panic. It was at that instant that McCoy decided he was no longer off duty.

"Easy . . . I'm Dr. McCoy. Is there something I can do for you?" he asked gently.

She had to lift her head to look at him as she was hunched over. "Yes," she said, gritting her teeth. "Perhaps there is. I seem to have developed this strange compulsion to double over. Do you think it might be significant?" She clearly had no intention of taking herself seriously.

"Might be." He took the arm that was not wrapped around the area of concern and helped her to an examination table. She would not lie down at first, but tried to sit up. McCoy gently kept pushing her back down. "Now, just lie there. Where does it hurt?"

"Three guesses," she said, patting her stomach. In the monitor's light, she looked even younger than she had in the lounge.

"Uh-huh. Can you describe the pain for me?"

"It hurts."

"I mean, is it stabbing, a dull ache . . ."

"It's sharp. It sort of burns."

An internal scan showed McCoy exactly what he expected. "It looks like you're working on an ulcer, my dear. For some reason, you've been producing too much stomach acid. If this had gone on much longer, you'd have a bona-fide hole in your gut. What I don't understand is why this didn't show up during an earlier checkup. Someone should have caught the beginnings of this long ago."

"I'm fast at everything," Anitra said.

"Well, you may be fast but you're going to need some medication," McCoy said. "I'm going to check your file. Lanter, isn't it?"

She partially sat up again and frowned at him. "Have we met?"

"I watched you play a little chess in the rec lounge. I can remember the name of anyone who can beat Spock—besides, it made me ten credits richer."

"Gambling," she said, her face twitching with the pain, but McCoy fancied he caught a bit of the glimmer in her eyes. "Really, Doctor. I'm shocked." She paused one beat for effect. "I netted a hundred."

McCoy grinned broadly as he accessed her file. "Lanter, Anitra, right?"

She nodded and bit her lip.

"Hold on," McCoy said. "I'm just checking to see if the medicine I'm about to prescribe is contraindicated." He bent down to read the terminal screen . . . and his smile quickly metamorphosed into a frown. "What the—"

"A problem?" Anitra asked, staring solemnly at the ceiling.

"Something wrong with the computer. This says it's your file, but the information—" McCoy broke off, confused.

"What does it say?"

"Your medical file lists you as a one-hundred-sixty-year-old Benecian slime worm with a history of prostate trouble. No allergies."

"That's absurd!" she protested. "I break out in hives every time I eat chocolate."

McCoy subjected her to his sternest gaze for a long time. "If you think this is funny, Ensign, think again. I'm not going to prescribe anything for you until I read your file. And what the devil are you doing monkeying around with those, anyway? I'd better not find any other files tinkered with—"

"You won't." She was sitting up now and tilted her chin upward. It gave her an almost feline, haughty look. "It can only be accessed under Lanter, Anitra M. Enter anything else and you get the Benecian."

"Thank you," McCoy said. He entered it. "That's much better." He scanned the file briefly and then went back into the lab. When he returned, he gave her a vial of pills. "Take one now."

Anitra swallowed one, closed her eyes and sighed as the muscles in her body relaxed in response to the absence of pain. When she looked at McCoy again, the light in her eyes had returned.

"I'd like to try to figure out how that ulcer got started," McCoy said. "I couldn't detect any physiological basis for the excess acidity. Is there any unusual stress that you've recently come under?"

"Swallowing acid comments," she said archly.

McCoy smiled faintly. "You know what I mean—the new job going all right and all that?"

"It's going great," she said.

"Which department?"

"Astrophysics. Research. Actually, things are sometimes slower in there than I'd like, but that's okay. Spock and I are working together on a project—particle physics, my one true love—so that keeps me interested."

"A project? On or off duty?"

"Off. We're hoping to publish a paper on our findings."

"How much free time do you spend on this project?"

"Not enough. I know what you're getting at with all this, Doctor. All I can say is, maybe it's just being assigned to a new ship. I don't find anything here particularly disturbing, and I enjoy working in my off-duty hours. I know you'll tell me all work and no play—but that's the way I've always lived. So don't worry." She sighed. "I'm sure I'll adjust."

"Wait a minute. I'm supposed to be reassuring *you.* Besides, I can't imagine anyone *wanting* to spend their off-duty time with Spock."

She cocked an eyebrow in perfect imitation. "Actually, he's a fascinating individual."

McCoy grimaced. "You *have* been around him too long, haven't you? Maybe you need to find other outside interests besides physics."

"Ah, but I do, Doctor." She smiled mysteriously. "I do. And Spock and I sometimes talk about things other than physics."

"Spock? Talk about something other than science?"

"Why not? He's been teaching me Vulcan philosophy and culture. He's even taking me to visit his family when we take shore leave."

McCoy heard a tiny internal alarm go off. "That's fine, but why don't you take some time off from the project? Meet some other people besides Spock—people your own age."

She frowned. "I don't understand. What does age have to do with anything?"

"You know . . . young men."

Her creamy complexion turned a delightful shade of pink. "Maybe I'm not interested, Doctor. I have far more important concerns right now, and frankly, I don't think it's any of your business. I've had enough of this kindly old doctor routine and your quaint, chauvinistic notions—"

In spite of himself, McCoy responded hotly to her sudden anger. "Now look here, I'm just trying to be helpful—"

"You've already helped enough," she said huffily, and, pills in hand, climbed off the exam table and headed for the door. "You just need to know when to stop."

"Well, I'll be . . ." McCoy said in amazement as the door closed behind her.

Amanda had not slept well; she had dreamed fitfully the night before, anxious dreams about Sarek and his brother, and a dead civilization. She glanced at the chronometer on the ceiling; it was early, but as always, Sarek's side of the bed was already empty.

Outside, the morning was gray, and the air still held

a hint of the evening chill that descended each night over the desert. Sarek was in the garden, as she had expected, but not at his usual place on the stone meditation bench. He stood looking down at the ground.

Amanda's mind at first refused to believe what she saw. Two of the five bushes she had planted the day before were uprooted, torn out of the ground, their bare, thorny limbs bent and broken. A sudden rage swelled up within her; in all her years on Vulcan, she had never seen the willful destruction of a thing of beauty.

"Who—what—did this?" she choked, her fists clenched.

Sarek studied his wife coolly. "A *chkariya,* most likely."

"A what?"

"Rather like a ferret." Sarek looked thoughtfully at the destruction and walked over to one of the bushes. He turned it over with his foot.

"We've never had them before! Why would it single out my rosebushes like this?" Amanda made a sweeping gesture at them.

"Chkariyas are not known for their logic."

His placid answer served as fuel for her anger. "Well, I don't care what they're known for. I want the damn things stopped, and I don't care how you do it."

Sarek gazed at her calmly. "Anger serves no useful purpose, my wife. The roses can be replaced."

"Not that easily," Amanda said, embarrassed by the fact that she was actually near tears. Why did the loss of two bushes bother her so? Sarek was right; they could be replaced. And three had survived. But it was just that the destruction of them seemed so—willfully evil, so intentionally aimed at her.

"I will buy a trap," said Sarek, "and tomorrow take the creature to the desert. Your other flowers will be safe, Amanda."

"Yes, of course," Amanda said automatically, but did not look at him; her eyes were fastened on the ruined bushes on the ground.

It wasn't like him at all. In the year she'd known him, al-B had never reported late for duty, not even by a minute. Tomson's first thought was that he was sick—too sick, maybe, to call in or answer the page. Her second thought was one that worried her even more: Moh was taking advantage of his new rank. She shook her head and dismissed it, although it still nagged in the back of her mind. She couldn't have been that mistaken about the person he was—especially now. No, something had to be wrong.

Tomson clicked off the intercom and bit her lip. If Moh were anywere on the ship, he would have answered by now. The nagging thought surfaced again: he doesn't think he has to. He knows you wouldn't report him—not only because of what it would do to his promotion, but because of what it would do to your credibility with the review board.

It struck her then: the transfer. Would he really jeopardize everything just to stay? He had kidded about it last night, kept repeating how he didn't want to leave her now . . . and her anxiety was replaced for a short while by anger. Pulling something like this would prove him to be more of a fool than she'd thought.

She looked over at Nguyen, who had reported in and was waiting patiently for her assignment. "Stay here for a few minutes," Tomson said. "If al-B reports in, page me."

It seemed only natural to look for him in his quarters. If he were elsewhere on the ship, Tomson reasoned, someone might see him and report that he was ignoring his page. It would be smarter just to ignore the intercom and the pages while laying low in his quarters.

When she got there, she pressed the buzzer. She was not at all surprised when no one answered. She leaned closer. "Al-B," she called, and put her hand on the door. To her surprise, it opened.

It was dark inside. Tomson fumbled for the light panel and pressed it. Seeing that the outer office was empty, she moved toward the darkened bedroom, and was just able to make out a human figure lying on the bed. She squared her shoulders. "Al-Baslama," she said sternly and turned on the light.

And began to scream and scream and scream, as though she would never stop.

Tomson was waiting in front of al-Baslama's quarters, paler than usual, her arms folded tightly, fighting to keep her composure.

"In there," she said to McCoy and Kirk. "Please try not to touch anything."

The dead man's body was stretched out on his bunk. McCoy was used to dead bodies, and Kirk had steeled himself for the sight of this one, but both of them flinched involuntarily. Tomson did not even try to look again; she had already forced herself to see more than she could bear. Mohamed al-Baslama had been beaten to death—not just once or twice in the strategic places, but over the entire surface of his body. His face was disfigured almost beyond recognition, the jaw and cheekbones broken. McCoy raised the dead man's tunic, and Kirk fought the desire to look away. The spleen had swollen the stomach to ghastly size, and the skin above it was mottled dark red and purple.

"Internal bleeding," McCoy said. "Probably the ultimate cause of death."

"Any idea who did this?" Kirk asked Tomson.

"A professional," she said. "Did you notice, no signs of a struggle? And al-Baslama was a damn good martial artsman. Not a hair, not a fingerprint, nothing out of place. I'm the only one who's been here, but I did a preliminary checkout. I have some people coming who'll go over this place with a fine-tooth comb. Al-B had a lot of friends in security." She faltered for a moment and looked away. "And Dr. McCoy needs to do an autopsy. So I can't really say we don't have any leads yet."

McCoy was muttering to himself. Kirk leaned over him. "Find anything unusual, Doctor?"

"If you want to call it that," McCoy said with disgust. He pointed at the dead man's hands. "Look there; every finger on both hands broken, smashed." He looked up at the captain. "Jim, this man was tortured to death."

The next day, McCoy caught Spock in the hall outside his quarters.

"I wonder if I could speak to you about Anitra Lanter."

"What is it you wish to discuss?" Spock asked.

"Last night she came to me complaining of severe stomach pains. It seems she's working on an ulcer."

McCoy imagined he detected a note of concern in Spock's voice. "Is the condition serious?"

"Not at this point, but if it doesn't improve, it could become that. What has me concerned is Anitra's . . ." McCoy tried to find the right word, ". . . lifestyle."

"That is none of my concern." Spock started to move away, but McCoy blocked him.

"It is very much your concern, Spock. A blind man could see that she's been your constant companion since she came on board. In fact, you two have spent every off-duty moment together."

"That is, as usual, a gross exaggeration, Doctor," Spock said in the long-suffering tone he used to explain the obvious to the unenlightened. "And I fail to see how my company could induce Dr. Lanter to develop an ulcer."

"Well, ulcers are caused by oversecretion of stomach acid, which is usually caused by an excess of stress—"

"I am constantly amazed, Doctor, by your ability to state the obvious."

"Dammit, Spock, let me finish. I'm simply trying to figure out what's causing the stress. Now I know that she's working on a project with you during her off-duty hours. Could it be that you're working her too hard?"

Spock frowned slightly. "I do not invoke the privilege of rank—we are merely two scientists working in our free time on a project of mutual interest. Dr. Lanter works as much as she cares to. I neither encourage nor discourage her."

"Well, frankly, I wish you would discourage her a little, Spock. I think she's suffering from overwork."

Spock raised an eyebrow. "That hardly seems my place, Dr. McCoy. If you, as her physician, feel that she should spend less time on the project, then you should tell her so."

"I did," McCoy muttered, "but I don't trust her to."

Spock made no reply, but turned to walk away.

"Wait, Spock, that's not all. . . . I don't know quite how to say this. . . ."

"That has never stopped you before."

The Vulcan was in rare form today. McCoy forced himself to ignore the remark, drew in a breath and said, "Look, I think she has a crush on you."

"A 'crush'?"

"Do you want me to explain it to you?"

"I am familiar with the idiom, Doctor. I was merely expressing . . . surprise that you would come to that conclusion."

"You wouldn't know a crush if it bit you. I'm telling you that this girl is in love with you. She spends every waking moment with you and I don't think it's healthy for her. It might be kinder to her if you could think up some excuses from time to time instead of spending every free moment working on the project together."

Spock was wearing that certain stone-faced expression that McCoy knew from experience meant he would get no cooperation. "I assure you that I am not completely insensitive to such situations, Doctor. I have encountered the problem in the past, but I have not perceived any such problem with Dr. Lanter."

McCoy could not believe him. "Spock, she told me

you've invited her to meet your family when we take shore leave. Don't you realize the significance of such an action?"

"Friendship," Spock said. "Any interpretation beyond that is merely wishful thinking on your part."

"Or on hers. She's young, Spock, and not all that mature. On Earth, when a man brings a woman home to meet his parents, it usually means that—"

Spock cut him off. "I am not taking her to Earth," he said evenly. "You are merely reading your own cultural interpretation into this."

"She's Terran, too," McCoy argued. "She's bound to come to the same—"

Spock cut him off smoothly. "I find this entire discussion entirely inappropriate, Dr. McCoy. Your questions merit no response except to say that you should not meddle in areas beyond your expertise."

"Why, you—" sputtered McCoy, but Spock had already turned on his heel and gone.

Tomson called to say that further investigation had yielded no leads.

Kirk's response was less than forgiving. "Lieutenant, I have four hundred crew members about to take shore leave for the first time in seven months. We have the option of canceling that leave or finding the killer. Do you understand?"

"Yes, sir," Tomson said stoutly. "Then the only suggestion I have, Captain, is that we run a verifier scan on all four hundred crew members."

"And our guests," Kirk said.

Tomson paused. "Sir . . . they're Vulcans."

"Well, if it's true that Vulcans can't lie, then they

have nothing to worry about. And Spock tells me that Vulcans can't be offended. Run the scan on them."

"Yes, sir."

Kirk stopped off at his quarters before going to the officers' mess. Somehow, a small drop of the murdered man's blood had stained his tunic, and he felt the need for a ritual cleansing before dinner. He stepped into the shower stall fully clothed, reached for the sonic controls—and then changed his mind. Today's circumstances called for a more therapeutic means of hygiene: hot water and steam. Kirk stripped, threw the tainted clothes out and closed the door behind him. The cubicle began to fill with white droplets of steam, and he let it continue until it was so dense he couldn't see his own hand in front of him.

He had lost men before, and al-Baslama's was not the first murder on board the *Enterprise* . . . but before, such things had always occurred under unusual circumstances, caused by external forces—spies, invaders, outsiders. Other than the Vulcans, there was no one to pin the guilt on, leaving the uncomfortable deduction that a crew member was responsible. Such a thing had never happened under his command before, and certainly he had never encountered a murder so maliciously committed.

Kirk closed his eyes and sighed, forcing his muscles to relax. He succeeded to a modest degree, and after a moment or two, he did something he had not done in years: he began to sing.

It was the time of the ship's day when the officers' mess was most crowded. McCoy had gotten his tray and was headed toward Scott's and Uhura's table when Anitra caught his eye and waved him over. She was sitting off to one side with Spock, and although McCoy was in no hurry to see the Vulcan after their most recent unpleasant encounter, he was far too intrigued to turn away.

Anitra greeted him with an enthusiastic smile; the sudden storm of temper in sickbay had apparently blown over without leaving any ill effects. But she had not forgotten it.

"I'd like to apologize for the other day," she said as McCoy took a seat next to her. "No hard feelings?"

"None at all," said McCoy. "I decided that your point was well taken."

"I think so," she said, but her eyes were playful.

McCoy gracefully ignored the remark, as Spock continued eating his meal on Anitra's other side, ignoring him. "How's the medication working out?"

Anitra and Spock exchanged a quick glance; obviously, there were things that she preferred to keep to herself. "Just great. Please, go ahead and eat."

McCoy hadn't touched his food. After al-Baslama's autopsy, he hadn't much of an appetite. Normally, such things never bothered him—in med school, he used to pride himself on his ability to eat lunch, a sandwich in one hand, while carving up a cadaver with the other—but it had never struck him as grisly, as this one had, possibly because none of the cadavers had been bludgeoned to death. . . . He smiled palely at his dinner. "Guess I'm just not as hungry as I thought."

"Want some of my fudge brownie?" Anitra wheedled. "It's awfully good."

He frowned. "I thought you were allergic to choc—"

He broke off, interrupted by the unlikely and painfully loud sound of off-key singing. "What the hell—" he began and then stopped, for by then he had recognized the captain's voice—as obviously had the rest of the crowd. After a moment of startled silence, titters began to flutter through the room. Only two of those seated did not share in the laughter—Spock and Anitra. And although Spock came alarmingly close to a double take, he recovered smoothly enough (since everyone was far too distracted to notice his reaction), and now simply sat, studying the reaction of the others. Anitra alone continued eating with gusto, unfazed, but grinning like a Cheshire cat.

"So do you want some or not?" she persisted, while McCoy gazed at her, dumbstruck.

Spock and Scott stood at attention. Kirk was in his quarters, now fully dressed, and in significantly less melodic voice. He paced back and forth in front of his officers.

"In answer to your question, sir," Scott said, his face twitching with the awful struggle to maintain decorum, "it was a simple microphone—something anyone could have planted. And it woulda been no trouble to hook in into the main intercom system."

Kirk stopped pacing and looked sourly at Scott. "No trouble. For you, perhaps, Scotty."

"Aye, sir." The subtlest twitch passed over the Scot's face.

"I must agree with the captain," Spock said. His

smoothly serious composure was in striking contrast to Scott's. "It would require no small amount of engineering talent to hook the microphone up to communications—"

"And pick the lock to my quarters. Who on this ship would have that kind of expertise?" Kirk demanded.

Spock shifted uncomfortably. "I would, sir."

"And I," Scott volunteered.

"That's very gallant of you gentlemen," Kirk said impatiently, "but since neither one of you has confessed to the crime, who does that leave us with?"

Spock and Scott eyed each other for a moment before Spock cleared his throat. "Lieutenant Uhura, sir, although it would be most out of character for her—"

"And?"

"And . . . a few other individuals in science and engineering."

"Who are they? I want to speak to them."

"I will . . . attempt to arrange it, sir," Spock said, knowing exactly who he needed to speak to, wondering if he could convince her to admit it.

The verifier scan showed nothing. Kirk consulted McCoy.

"Can anyone fool a verifier scan, Doctor?"

McCoy waxed philosophic. "Well, now, some would tell you no. But maybe . . . well, maybe someone with a pathological condition, who was convinced he was telling the truth, could fool the scanner."

Kirk nodded. "And, of course, you have no one

with a psychological profile who would fit this description?"

McCoy frowned. "If someone like that got through the academy and past me, they're in the wrong business. They ought to take up the theater, and I ought to be drummed out of my job."

"Could someone—formerly healthy—experience a personality change that would permit them to do what someone did to al-Baslama?"

"God knows we've seen enough types of space madness, Jim. I'd say it's possible."

"Then I'd like you to update your files, Doctor. I want a recent psychological analysis of everyone on board this ship."

McCoy started to grin, but it faded quickly when he realized that the captain was not smiling. "You're not kidding, are you?"

"I'm not kidding."

"Do you have any idea how long that would take? We'd have to pull double shifts in sickbay just to get it done before the end of the month—"

"Then pull double shifts. But I want it done before we go on shore leave."

McCoy grimaced. "No problem, Captain. There's nothing I like better than trying to pick one sadist out of four hundred and twenty crew members."

The day passed without incident, and Amanda forgot about the roses until she went out into the garden shortly after sunset, when the heat had broken. The sight of two empty holes where the bushes had been was an unpleasant reminder, but she noted with satisfaction that Sarek had kept his promise—a small trap, a square box with an entrance but no exit, sat next to the remaining rosebushes, no doubt loaded with chka-riya pheromones.

She heard a rustle behind her and turned to see someone hidden in the shadows at the other end of the garden, near the tall bushes. Her heart beat faster until she realized it was Silek; she drew a small sigh and smiled. He seemed almost startled himself, but he walked toward her.

"I see that two of your roses are missing."

"Furry vandals," she said. "I take it your presentation at the academy went well."

Silek nodded.

"And that you slept well last night."

Amanda watched his expression with fascination; like his brother, Silek could convey wry amusement without moving a single muscle in his face. "Do you wish an honest answer, my lady Amanda, or the expected one?"

Her eyes saddened. "I wouldn't blame you, Silek, if you didn't. So many things happen in thirty-eight years, so many changes. I didn't even know that you were married, and now Sarek tells me that you recently lost your wife."

Privately, Silek was amused by her use of a very Terran idiom. Humans. Their fear of death was so great they could not force themselves to speak its name, lest it take notice of them. He wondered how one might literally lose one's wife—misplace her, per-haps. Aloud he said, "Yes. We married shortly after we met. She was a researcher on the Hydrilla project. I'm sorry that you did not have the opportunity to meet T'Ylle." He thought of T'Ylle here and wondered what Amanda would make of her—certainly two women were never more opposite. Amanda was everything open and warm and forthright, while T'Ylle was cool, retiring, always watching and weighing. . . .

"Was she ill?"

"The official cause was listed as an accident," said Silek. He was staring in the direction of the sun, although it had already disappeared below the horizon.

"You say that as though you don't believe it was."

"It was not," Silek said, still watching the nonexistent sunset. "T'Ylle was intentionally killed." Why he chose to tell Amanda now he did not know. It was foolish, illogical, for it could accomplish no aim save to upset her. Amanda did not need to know, yet it somehow seemed rude to refuse to explain further. And perhaps there was some sort of relief in finally being able to voice it, to say the dreadful words aloud, to another who would listen.

Amanda was shocked speechless for a moment. "I thought the expedition was all Vulcan."

"Forgive me." Silek returned to his senses. "I am a poor guest to so disturb my hostess. I have no proof to back my claim. Let us discuss it no further."

But the look of anxiety in Amanda's eyes reminded him very much of something he had found in T'Ylle's cool brown ones shortly before her death, the unspoken fear she had kept from him, to protect him, until it was far too late. . . .

The ground had given way, Starnn had claimed, given way and crumbled beneath their feet—and T'Ylle had fallen from the overhang onto the rocks below. Fallen, Silek recalled grimly, but not without assistance.

He wanted to warn Amanda now . . . but it was still early. Such a warning now would only serve to confuse and terrify. Perhaps he knew what he had to do to set things right.

Out of politeness, Amanda did not press him, though there were many questions she wanted to ask. Instead, she stood and held him with that troubled gaze.

Silek spoke again. "Our expedition to Hydrilla was successful, but many strange things happened on the last planet—on Beekman. Three of our party were killed—T'Ylle and two others. All died under unusual circumstances—all 'accidents.' Some of the people on the expedition seemed to—change—as a result. Starnn, for example."

"He's elderly," Amanda said. "And he lost a daughter."

"True." Silek suddenly felt tired of discussing the subject. He looked down at the trap Sarek had set. "What type of animal are you expecting another visit from?"

"A chkariya," Amanda said, accepting the change of subject with an insincere cheerfulness, her eyes still troubled. "It pulled two bushes right out of the ground last night and somehow managed to snap the branches right in two. Terran that I am, I hope it got a mouthful of thorns."

Silek frowned. "You are sure a chkariya did that? I did not think them capable. . . ."

"Sarek thinks it might be. Whatever it is, I'm going to stop it."

54

Silek finally looked at her. "For your sake, I hope you do."

She smiled at him. "I'll see you at dinner."

Silek waited until he was sure that she had gone inside the house before he went back over to the bushes. The small mammal lay half buried in the sand, its teeth bared in a death scream. Its neck had been snapped, and its legs dangled from its limp body at unnatural angles. Silek did not doubt that the animal had been tortured before it was killed.

It was starting again, just as it had started on Beekman's Planet.

Chapter Three

"COMING INTO ORBIT around Vulcan, Captain," Sulu announced. On the screen was a red giant of a planet.

Kirk snapped off the intercom on the arm of the con. He was not at all surprised when McCoy called to say that working round the clock, the medical staff had managed to psychoscan only half the crew, and of those, all were normal.

"So much for shore leave," Kirk said quietly.

The remark had been too soft for others on the bridge to overhear—except, of course, for Spock. The Vulcan walked over to Kirk's side.

"Captain," he said in a low voice, "for one guilty of murder charges, Vulcan would be a most difficult planet to escape from, particularly if security central were alerted to the problem and landing parties required to stay in groups of three or four."

Kirk grunted. "If they were required to stay together the entire time—it might work." He smiled up at his first officer. "A logical solution, Mr. Spock, but I might be tempted to think that you're trying to convince me not to cancel shore leave for purely ulterior motives."

Spock's expression was one of mild shock. "Sir, I was merely trying to be of assistance. . . ."

Kirk laughed briefly. "So be it. We're long overdue for a little R and R. Groups of four—no one is to be alone, not even for an instant."

"That," said Spock, "is likely to prove interesting." He returned to his station and bent over his viewer.

"Maybe it won't be so bad," Kirk mused, watching the planet rotate on the view screen. "Is there any place you would recommend, Spock, for out-of-town-ers looking for some purely human forms of entertainment?"

Spock did not answer. He remained bent over his viewer.

"Spock? Is there something wrong?" Kirk got out of his chair and went over to Spock's station.

"There appear to be some abnormalities with Vulcan's atmosphere," Spock said, distracted, without looking up.

"Abnormalities?"

"It cannot be the instruments," Spock said. "I just ran diagnostics on them; they're in perfect working order. As I know the exact composition of Vulcan's atmosphere, I was scanning to test their calibration. I often do so as a matter of procedure—"

"What sort of abnormalities, Spock?"

Spock looked up and sighed. "My scanner registers the atmosphere as unusually dense. According to computer analysis, the chemical composition and consistency indicates that the atmosphere has become . . . split-pea soup."

"Split-pea soup?" Kirk asked.

"There is something I must talk to you about," Spock said. He and Anitra sat in the office in his quarters.

"Then talk, sir," she said.

"I do not understand the purpose of practical joking."

"It's funny."

Spock focused his gaze on her intently, and she shifted her chair; if she didn't know him better, she might think he was trying to intimidate her with that peculiar, nonthreatening but nonetheless frightening way Vulcans had. "You might think such jokes humorous, Dr. Lanter, but they can lead to serious outcomes."

"Such as?" Anitra asked coolly.

"Changing the readings of instruments at critical times when quick decisions must be made could lead to life-threatening situations. And personally humiliating the captain serves no purpose except to infuriate him and, should you be discovered to be the perpetrator, damage your career in Star Fleet."

"What makes you think it's me?"

Spock stared at her without answering, and she felt herself flushing in spite of herself.

"And besides," she said, "maybe I'm not that concerned about my career."

"I am at present," Spock said. "We cannot afford any interference with our mission."

"All right, then, I apologize," she said, straight-faced, then she suddenly covered her mouth with her hand. "But you have to admit, it was funny."

Spock held her with that stony stare. "It is not necessary to apologize to me."

"Then what do you want?"

"Apologize to the captain."

She blanched and lowered her hand. "You just said that we couldn't risk any interference—"

"Ensign, he has ordered me to find the perpetrator. I could have told him that I knew who it was, but I would prefer you went to him voluntarily."

"I see." She considered it for a moment. "I suppose in that case, I volunteer."

Kirk was just about to step into the shower fully clothed—the sonic, that is, since he hadn't resorted to water showers since the fateful incident—when the buzzer sounded.

It was Anitra Lanter.

"Come in, Ensign." For a minute, he could not piece together why she was there.

"I've come to confess, Captain," she said.

She seemed contrite enough, but there was a hint of a smirk in her eyes that aggravated the hell out of him. "I see. Would you like to explain to me why you did it, Ensign?"

She looked at the floor. Kirk was not sure if it was out of shame and regret, or simply an attempt to hide those dancing eyes. "I suppose I thought it was— funny, sir."

"Funny," he echoed tonelessly. "Do you realize that you could be charged with breaking and entering a senior officer's quarters? And sabotage, for tampering with the communications board and Mr. Spock's computers?"

"Yes, sir," she said in what Kirk judged to be a sincerely meek voice.

"I could very easily slap you with ten demerits, Ensign, and have you decommissioned. Do you understand that?"

"Yes, sir."

"But that would be a waste of a very ingenious officer. Since you appear to be so good at manipulating the hardware around here, I'm going to give you a little project that you can do in your off-duty hours, to keep you out of trouble. Engineer Scott needs some help overhauling the engines. Have you ever overhauled engines, Ensign?"

"No, sir. I guess I've just been lucky," she answered, without a trace of impudence.

Kirk was beginning to experience some degree of satisfaction. For an experienced engineer, an overhaul might take a day—for an engineering genius like Scotty, several hours. A neophyte—ah, a neophyte might well take forever. "It's a project that usually requires two men and a full day's work. I'm sure those men would appreciate getting off early for shore leave. I'm going to let you do their work, Ensign—but you are not relieved of any of your other duties. You are to do it only when you are off duty. Understood?"

"Understood. If I finish in time, may I take shore leave, sir?" she asked timidly.

Kirk smiled sardonically. "Of course, Ensign." By that time, leave on Vulcan would be nothing more than a memory—one that she would definitely not share with the rest of the crew.

She smiled suddenly and brilliantly at him. "Is that all, sir?"

"That's all," Kirk said smugly. She would soon find it to be more than enough.

Each day the trap came up empty, while the rose-bushes were destroyed methodically, one by one. Two more dead animals were discovered and put into the incinerator.

One evening after the guests had retired, Amanda went to speak with her husband. He had not gone to bed, of course, but was sitting in his study. It seemed he never came to bed at all these days.

The door to Sarek's study opened in response to his wife's voice. Sarek watched her as she came in, and knew that she was quite agitated, although anyone else would not have been able to tell from her perfectly composed movements. Only her eyes betrayed her, and her lips, which were pressed together somewhat more tightly than usual.

"Sarek," she began in a voice deceptively calm to the ear, "have you moved your father's *ahn vahr* for any reason?" The double-edged sword had been in Sarek's family for centuries and was displayed in a place of honor on the wall of the central room, an ancient reminder of Vulcan's warrior past. *Please*, Amanda's eyes begged numbly. *Say yes. Say you took it to have it polished.*

"No," said Sarek. "Is it missing?"

His wife's lips compressed even more. "Come with me," she said resolutely. "You must see this."

Without question, Sarek rose and followed his wife to the central room. The ahn vahr was, indeed, missing from its customary place. But something even more bizarre . . . the portrait of Amanda and her son hung in its usual place—upside down.

"Who would do this?" Amanda whispered. "Why would anyone here do something like this?" This was Vulcan, not Earth. Nothing irrational or insane had happened here in five thousand years, except in the tourist quarter . . . but not here.

Sarek did not answer her. He walked over to the portrait and righted it, and after a time, he said, "I will implement the security screens and see to it that our guests are given the code."

"Not Starnn," Amanda said quickly, in spite of herself. "Just Silek. Starnn doesn't need it; he always comes home with you, anyway."

Sarek studied the bare spot on the wall. "As you wish, Amanda."

No doubt it was the rigorous code of Vulcan hospitality that compelled Spock to invite Kirk and McCoy to visit his parents' home in ShiKahr. Kirk had accepted out of politeness, although he made it clear to Spock that at least a few hours' leave would be dedicated to less civilized pursuits. McCoy accepted out of a desire to keep an eye on Anitra; upon learning she would not be coming, he stewed silently on his transporter pad, thinking of the hours that he could have spent in one of the tourist bars in the capital.

Scott was just on the verge of beaming them down when Anitra entered the transporter room. She gave them all a sprightly nod and took her place on the platform next to Spock.

"Ensign Lanter." Kirk glowered at her. "I thought we had an agreement."

She blinked innocently at him. "Is there a problem, sir? I thought you said that when I was finished overhauling the engines—"

"Aye," Scott spoke up with enthusiasm before the captain could protest. "And I'd forgotten to thank ye, sir. It's glad I am you sent her to help out. I had no idea the ensign here was such an old salt at overhaulin' engines. . . ."

"I'm not, Mr. Scott," Anitra said quickly before Kirk could protest, but not before he shot her a withering look. "I swear, that's the first time I've ever helped to overhaul an engine."

"You'll never get me to believe it," Scott said, addressing Kirk. "Captain, the woman's a phenomenon. She never asked a single question, just seemed to know what to do before I could get the words out of my mouth. And she did the job exactly as I woulda done it myself. Simply uncanny. It took half the time. I usually have to repeat myself a hundred times before a greenhorn understands what's goin' on."

"I see," Kirk said heavily, without taking his eyes off of Lanter.

"Well, I'm most grateful, sir, for your sendin' Dr. Lanter to help out."

Anitra smiled her brilliant smile at them all; if there had been a trace of smugness in it, Kirk would have ordered her off the platform. As it was, he resigned himself to a stony, disapproving glare.

For some reason, Scott was unable to get a fix on the interior of Spock's home, and they were required to beam down outside. This caused Kirk and McCoy to put an immediate, silent curse on Star Fleet and Komack in particular, for the climate could not, even with the most generous interpretation, be called inviting. It was early evening, just before sunset, the time when the afternoon winds were in full force. The breezes, if they could be called by such a gentle name, gave no relief from the 115° heat; indeed, they seemed hotter than the still air, and served only to punctuate the heat all the more, and to whip up sand, stinging human eyes.

McCoy wondered aloud how such an advanced civilization could still be afflicted with sand streets.

Spock paid him no heed, but held his hand before a small metal plate on the great stone wall which stood before them. He seemed rather surprised when nothing happened.

"This may explain the problem with the transporter, Captain. I believe that the security system is on."

Kirk wiped the perspiration from his forehead and left his hand there to shield his eyes from the sand. "I thought you said they were expecting us."

Spock shrugged. "They are. Most unusual. My parents haven't used the security system for twenty years."

"I hope you haven't forgotten the code," McCoy raised his voice in a rather ungracious tone over the howling wind. "I'd like to get out of this mess." Under his breath he muttered, "Hell of a place for R and R."

Spock turned his face toward him and arched a brow, but did not answer. Instead, he touched the four corners of the metal plate in what seemed to be a random fashion. The massive gate slid open.

The outside of the house was typically Vulcan in design—an unimpressive dome-shaped structure, the same as all Vulcan homes, whether they were built two thousand years ago, a hundred years ago or yesterday. Inside, the humans noticed with immediate relief that the house was cooler and not as dry—indeed, it was almost comfortable for a human, although not quite as cool as they would have liked. Naturally, thought Kirk, a human lives here, too.

They walked through a long foyer into a large, open room, which was evidently used for entertaining guests.

"Wait here," Spock told them, then disappeared.

Kirk smiled; the house rather reminded him of his first officer. All Vulcan on the outside, but inside, there was definitely a human's touch: an old upright piano, a comfortable-looking sofa of decidedly Terran design, and on the wall, near displays of fierce-looking Vulcan weaponry, a portrait of mother and son.

Spock returned shortly. He wore a slight frown, which indicated that things were not as he had expected to find them. "I know that my mother is tutoring at this time. However, I had expected my father and some house guests to be present. Perhaps they were detained."

Anitra was staring dreamily at the portrait. "Is this your mother?"

Spock nodded. "Twenty-six years ago."

"She's very beautiful."

Spock grunted assent.

"The polite thing to do is thank her, Spock," said McCoy.

Spock raised his eyebrows in mild surprise. "I had

no hand in it, Dr. McCoy. I can scarcely take credit." He looked distractedly at the wall for a moment. "Odd . . ."

"What is it, Spock?" asked Kirk. "Something missing?"

"Yes . . . an antique. Perhaps my parents took it to be repaired. But I am failing in my duties as host. Please, sit down. Doctor, I am sure you would appreciate something alcoholic to drink."

McCoy sat on the couch, surprised. "You mean, your parents stock liquor?"

"They entertain frequently. And my mother has been known to imbibe occasionally. Whiskey? And you, Captain—a brandy?"

Kirk and McCoy smiled and shrugged at each other from across the couch before nodding. Spock playing bartender. Perhaps this wouldn't be so unpleasant after all.

"Dr. Lanter?"

Anitra had wandered over to the far end of the room and stood gazing out of the window that overlooked the garden. "Nothing for me, thanks," she said cheerfully.

Spock left to get their drinks.

"You should see the garden," Anitra said with her back to them. "It's incredibly lush compared to the desert out there. . . ." She broke off, her back straightening suddenly, strangely.

"What is it?" McCoy asked.

"I think I see someone out there."

"You wouldn't happen to be pulling anyone's leg, would you, Ensign?" Kirk's tone was cool.

She turned toward them, and after a glance at her

expression, both men jumped off the couch and went to the window.

"Over there," Anitra pointed, "in the bushes."

"Spock," Kirk called.

Spock returned, drinks in hand. They did not need to say anything to him. He followed their gaze to the window and looked outside.

"Captain, would you stay here with Anitra? Doctor, would you mind accompanying me?"

McCoy knew, of course, why he was being asked to go along. People who were alive did not lie motionless like that, and certainly not in thorn-covered bushes.

It did not surprise McCoy when he knelt down to find that the man was dead; nor, for some reason, did he feel any real sense of shock to find that the man had died as a result of repeated stab wounds. What startled him was that the Vulcan was a dead ringer for Spock, forty years from now.

He looked up at Spock from under lowered lids. "A relative of yours?"

Spock nodded. "I believe he is—was—my uncle." Silek's nephew studied him quietly for the first time. His face was composed, although covered with bloody scratches where he had fallen against the last remaining rosebush, and his wounds, mercifully, could not be clearly seen for all the blood.

"The ahn vahr," Spock said suddenly.

"The what?"

"The weapon missing from the wall. It could have been used to inflict his wounds."

McCoy looked up at him. "Do you know why anyone would want to murder your uncle?"

* * *

Sarek and Amanda had returned home, and a representative of Vulcan security had come . . . only then had anyone thought to look for Starnn. He lay on the floor in the guest room, toppled over from the kneeling position of ritual suicide, the ahn vahr still in his heart. The security representative requested the ahn vahr as well as the two bodies for examination. It was assumed that traces of Silek's blood would be found on the sword; nevertheless, she also respectfully requested that the landing party remain on Vulcan until the following day, when the investigation would be completed. In other words, as McCoy put it, they were not to leave town, the one thing the landing party wanted to do, not wishing to disturb the family's grief. And Amanda was clearly stricken, although she did not weep (at least, not where she could be seen or heard). Sarek, on the other hand, accepted his brother's death calmly.

And so the landing party spent the night—Anitra in one guest room, Kirk and McCoy in another, Spock in his old room. Under the circumstances, no one slept well.

Anitra dreamed that night—dreamed of murder, of the old Vulcan with the white hair and the sword through his heart, of Spock's uncle with tiny bloody scratches across his face. She was awakened not by the dreams, but by a strange noise—an internal humming, like the drone of thousands of wings beating in unison. She felt rather than heard them, but the source of the silent vibration was definitely external. It pulled her from her bed and led her into the spacious central area.

From the garden window she could see the stars shining clearly, and she paused for a moment to locate Sol. It was almost too weak to be seen by the naked eye, but it was there. On Earth it was impossible to see Eridani without aid, in part because of the brightness of the moon. But here the stars were glorious, for no moonlight detracted from their brilliance; on the other hand, the lack of it made it difficult for her to find her way in the dark. She walked, barefoot, with measured, silent steps, one hand held out in front to save her from colliding with the furniture, for she knew that the ears of some sleepers here were far more sensitive than her own.

She crossed the central room until she stood in front of a door, the edges of which glowed faintly in the darkness. Her pulse quickened. She was at once certain that inside lay what had awakened her. She put a hand on the door, gently, so that it would not misinterpret the touch as a desire to enter, and closed her eyes. *They* were here, in this room.

The sudden sensation of a presence in the nearby darkness startled her so that she whirled around, drawing in her breath sharply. The face of the Vulcan was obscured by darkness, but she could sense Spock's presence.

"What we're looking for is here," she whispered just audibly enough for him to hear.

"You are quite certain?"

She nodded, knowing that he was accustomed to the darkness and could see her quite easily.

"Why would it still be here, with Starnn dead?"

"I don't know, but it's here." She turned and faced

the door. "There's no one—at least, no person—inside. I'd like to investigate."

Spock would have liked to disagree, but could find no logical argument. Anitra moved so that the door to Sarek's study glided open. She walked inside with Spock close behind her.

The light was off in the study, but its entirety was dimly lit by the feeble luminescence of the small black ellipse on Sarek's desk.

"There," Anitra said, her large eyes focused on it. "In that."

"Be careful," said Spock, but Anitra was too fascinated to hear him. As she neared the object, the glow slowly flickered and began to recede toward it.

When the light had died away completely, the box began to open.

Anitra's eyes snapped away and found Spock's. "Get out of here," she hissed. "NOW."

They both bolted out the door. Anitra gasped as she landed directly in a steely pair of arms, recoiling immediately.

Sarek was fully dressed, as though he had not been to bed at all. He stared intently at them both, and at the open door to the study where the faint light emanated once again.

Don't look at him. The terrified thought passed through Spock's mind, and although it was not his own, the urgency of it was such that he obeyed.

"Dr. Lanter was unable to sleep," he said to his father with respectfully downcast eyes. "I heard a noise and came to investigate."

Sarek's voice was cold. "She should not wander

at night, considering what has happened here recently."

"I won't," Anitra said in a small voice. She turned and made a swift retreat toward the guest room. Spock bowed slightly to his father and followed her.

Sarek stared after the two of them for a moment and then went inside the study.

"I'm sorry."

Anitra and Spock were inside the guest room with the light on.

"Why do you apologize?" he asked. "We were able to escape safely, thanks to your alerting me. And it is not your fault that the evil has invaded my parents' household."

Anitra's voice was soft and husky. "More than you know, Spock."

Spock looked at her questioningly, although he had already guessed what was coming.

"I'm sorry, Spock. Whoever we spoke to tonight . . . isn't your father anymore."

Spock folded his arms calmly, but Anitra knew him well enough to know he would have reacted much the same to a heavy blow to his stomach. "Perhaps I suspected as much." He took a deep breath. "Although I'd hoped that I was wrong. This changes our plans."

"No it doesn't. Not yet, anyway. We're still going to the academy tomorrow."

"My mother," Spock said swiftly, firmly, "must be warned. She will have to leave. It isn't safe for her to remain."

"If she leaves, Sarek will know that she knows and come after her. And he'll deduce that we told her. Right now, he still doesn't suspect us. He only knows that we were drawn for some reason to the study. We can't risk it. Not yet." She folded her arms in unconscious imitation of him.

"But the danger . . ."

"Only to those who know or suspect. Your uncle suspected and warned Star Fleet. For that, he was killed. Do you want that to happen to your mother? To us?"

Spock looked intently at a point on the far wall and after a time said, "The moment we learn there is a threat to Amanda's safety . . ."

"We'll take care of it. Until then, we speak to no one."

"Very well." He shot her a dark glance that she could not interpret, then left.

Apparently, they were not the only ones suffering from insomnia, for McCoy stood waiting in the hallway.

"I thought I heard something," he said quietly. "But I'd convinced myself it was an auditory hallucination. A little late to be discussing physics, isn't it, Spock?"

Spock attempted to walk past him without acknowledgment, but McCoy stepped in front of him.

"Don't you realize how this looks, Spock?" His tone was sarcastic, but there was a razor-sharp edge to it that Spock was unable to interpret for a moment.

"I have nothing to explain to you, Doctor," he said, and pushed past him. McCoy remained in the hallway for a few moments, his eyes glittering jealously.

*　　*　　*

Vulcan security was as good as its word—the next morning, after a few questions, the landing party was free to go. It was no small measure of irritation to McCoy that only the humans were required to take a verifier scan.

"He's half human," the doctor said irritably to the officer operating the scanner, and thrust a thumb at Spock. "Doesn't that make him capable of at least exaggeration?"

With inscrutable Vulcan wisdom, the officer decided that the question was unworthy of reply.

They left Amanda and Sarek to their grief. Spock offered to take Anitra on a tour of the Vulcan Science Academy, which she accepted enthusiastically, despite McCoy's attempts to convince her otherwise. He and Jim were headed for one of the tourist bars in ShanaiKahr.

Amanda sat up, mysteriously jolted from sleep, and at the same instant was painfully disappointed to find herself awake. She had been plagued by insomnia since Silek's death, too horrified by the thought of how he had died, at what Starnn had become, to relax. Now, in the afternoon, sleep had come upon her at last, and just as quickly, slipped away.

The book she had been reading was still on her lap— an old paper book bound in cloth and leather. Her library was always filled with the comforting smell of dust and old paper, for the tall shelves in the library were lined with hundreds of antique books. The book in question had been a childhood favorite, and she had never tired of reading it—until now. Sighing, she shut it and put it back on the shelf, looking for something different to catch her interest. She ran her fingers over the backs of the books, but nothing appealed to her. Disgusted, she sat back in her chair, now completely wide awake.

And then her eye caught the title of the volume that rested on the small table next to the chair. *Letters from the Earth*. She had carefully set it aside there so that she might remember to read it next; perhaps her subconscious had refused to register the book's existence until now.

She picked it up and ran her hand over the gilt and leather cover, smiling sadly, touched that Silek had remembered her fondness for such things. There was no need to open the book at the middle and turn the pages back one by one; the spine had already been cracked once and repaired, and the pages were limp from centuries of being handled. Sad and warmed at the same time, Amanda began to read.

After the Table of Contents, before Chapter One, a slip of paper slid out and gracefully floated to the floor. Amanda leaned forward to pick it up, thinking it to be a used bookmark or an old letter. But the paper was crisp and new:

My lady Amanda,

This is the first time that I shall write you, and the last. I have found Starnn murdered, and know that my own time approaches. Do not grieve for me.

What I tell you is the truth, and regardless of how unbelievable it sounds, it must be acted upon quickly, without panic. The evil that destroyed Hydrilla has survived to infect Starnn. T'Ylle discovered this, but paid with her life. It is to my [the word here was archaic, and Amanda guessed it to mean "sorrow"] that I brought the evil into your household.

You must leave Sarek quickly, immediately, and give this note to the authorities. Do not confront him, or you shall meet with the gravest consequence.

Live long and prosper, sister.

Silek

Amanda rose, too numbed for thought or reason, and went into her bedroom. There her husband slept for the first time in several days, and she stood next to the bed, watching him, unthinking, unfeeling, as his chest rose and fell in slow, regular intervals. He stirred in his sleep and threw a hand across his forehead; in the gray light, she saw that his hands and wrists had been scratched.

With some quiet, detached part of her brain, she wondered how Sarek had gotten the scratches.

A logical explanation, her mind chattered furiously, there must be a perfectly logical explanation. . . .

And the quiet, detached part of her again asked, who killed Silek if Starnn had died first?

A different part of her brain answered, a part that seemed to be swelling with panic and threatening to burst. It spoke not with words, but a picture: she and Silek in the garden, Amanda laughing and saying, "I hope it got a mouthful of thorns."

Cold panic broke through her outer calm, and she felt a sudden urge to scream. Instead, she stole quietly from the room and back to the library. She went immediately to the view screen and tried, with trembling hands, to conjure the proper frequency, but it was not one that she called often. After several desperate, unsuccessful tries, the static ceased.

"This is Amanda Grayson on the planet Vulcan hailing the U.S.S. *Enterprise*."

"Enterprise. Lieutenant Uhura here."

"Get me Commander Spock, please. It's urgent."

"Ma'am, Commander Spock is still on the planet surface. Would you like us to locate him for you?"

A fist of crushing strength closed on Amanda's wrist. "Tell them no," Sarek said softly.

"No," she told Uhura.

Chapter Four

"HOW DO YOU intend to access the information?" Anitra asked. They were in Sarek's office in the new physics wing of the academy, and behind them the door was closed. Spock sat at the terminal, entering data while she leaned over him and squinted at the screen.

"Very simply," Spock said. "Security records are public domain." He leaned back as the screen filled with hieroglyphics.

Anitra frowned. "My Vulcan isn't that good."

"Since the return of the expedition, eleven murders." Spock keyed in a few more symbols and the screen shifted again.

"Planetwide?" Anitra asked.

Spock nodded. "Seven of those occurred in the tourist quarter, but the rest were Vulcan fatalities."

"Amazing," Anitra said. "Four Vulcans murdered in that period of time. In one city on Earth, more than that would be killed in one day."

"However, on Vulcan this is critically significant, given that these are the first murders to occur outside the tourist quarter in a thousand years." Spock peered at the screen again. "Two of those we already know of, but two others occurred in the towns of SriKahr and SuraKahr." He spoke a brief sentence in Vulcan into the computer, then turned to her. "I am checking for the names of those in the expedition." The screen flashed and changed before him. "Yes, as I thought. These are hometowns of Hydrillan-expedition members."

"Get the names. I'd be interested to know if they were the ones on board ship when al—"

The beep from Spock's communicator interrupted her; Spock answered. "Spock here."

"Lieutenant Uhura here, Mr. Spock. Your mother just contacted the ship, asking for you. She said it was extremely urgent. I told her that you were still on the planet surface and offered to find you, but she broke off communications rather abruptly. She sounded a little strange, so I thought I'd better contact you."

Spock stood up. "You did the right thing, Lieutenant. Thank you. I'll contact her."

"No problem, sir."

Spock snapped his communicator shut and turned to Anitra. "Remain here."

"No." Anitra folded her arms and set her chin with a determination as strong as the Vulcan's. "You need me there. You know that; you'd be as good as helpless without me."

"Not entirely helpless . . . while my telepathic skills are modest compared to yours, they still afford me some degree of protection against the creatures. And remember, this is my family. I am more sensitive to their thoughts."

"Perhaps no longer your family," Anitra murmured,

her face white. "Perhaps no longer their thoughts . . ."

"Admittedly, your presence would be a definite advantage." He held her eyes intently. "But your survival is crucial to this mission, and Star Fleet has put the onus of your safety on me. I cannot let you come. The risk is too great."

"You know that you can stop these things from spreading without me," Anitra said, but her tone was unconvincing. She lowered her head, unable to come up with a better counterargument.

"Perhaps," Spock answered, "but your death would greatly reduce Star Fleet's chances of success. And I would prefer at this point to keep the odds in our favor."

"We can't risk losing you, either, Spock. Promise that you'll contact me if you run into a serious problem."

He nodded, knowing that she was not speaking of the communicator. "Perhaps it would be safer for you not to remain alone here at the academy, where you are too obvious. It would be wiser for you to join the captain and the doctor." And, he reflected silently, it might get McCoy off his back.

"A tourist bar?" Anitra grimaced in disbelief.

"Who are you?" Amanda wheeled on her captor in what she knew to be a doomed attempt at bravado. "Where is my husband?"

"I am here, my wife," Sarek replied calmly.

She responded with haughty coolness worthy of a Vulcan. "You aren't Sarek. Whoever you are, whatever you are, I don't know, but I can sense that he's not here. What have you done with him?"

Sarek's face tightened suddenly in a grin—a grimace more than a smile. "He is here, my lady, but . . . indisposed. At the moment, he cannot speak to you."

Up to that moment, Amanda had not truly believed the evidence of her senses. Now her heart froze.

He moved closer to her, and she found herself pulling away until her back pressed against the spines of the books on the shelves. He neared until she felt his breath upon her face, and then he laughed at her, a horrible sound, so horrible that she covered her ears with her hands.

"*You* . . . killed Silek and Starnn," she said, but she no longer had control of her voice; like a dreamer, she screamed and heard it emerge from her throat something less than a whisper.

The creature emitted a low rumble and then a deep whine that intensified until she could no longer bear it. When it spoke again, the voice was low, rasping, no longer Sarek's.

"*We* . . . killed them. Sarek was rather distraught. He knows what has happened; he even knows we are talking to you now, and he is most distressed." It chuckled cruelly. "Starnn was one of ours, but no longer necessary. And Silek . . ." Sarek's eyes had begun to burn with an unnatural fire. "Silek had become a threat."

It moved even nearer to her, and smiled its horrible smile. "Just as you are now, my dear." It raised Sarek's finger and ran it as gently as a caress along the length of Amanda's neck, up under her chin. She tensed, unable to suppress a moan of revulsion.

"What shall we do with you, my dear?" it crooned.

*   *   *

Kirk never really understood how the fight began. He and McCoy weren't exactly drunk, merely well oiled by the time Anitra joined them at the bar in the center of ShanaiKahr's tourist quarter. The bar was just like any other bar in a large city with a major spaceport—crowded, dark, mercifully cool—but definitely much cleaner. There were no Vulcans inside—the proprietor was Rigellian—although Kirk noticed the Vulcan security officer conspicuously standing just outside the entrance, his sensitive ears on the alert for sounds of a brawl beginning between outworlders.

"Well, look who's here," McCoy drawled; the thickness of his Georgia accent was directly proportionate to the amount of alcohol he consumed, and at the moment it was rapidly growing more distinct. "We certainly weren't expecting you."

Anitra grinned, her face alive, mercurial, as she slid into the booth and surveyed her surroundings.

The barmaid had thrown a napkin onto the table before Anitra had settled herself in. "What'll it be?"

"It's such a pleasure to know there are people on this planet who speak in contractions," McCoy sighed.

"What are you having?" Anitra leaned over the table to look at their drinks.

"I have finally convinced the captain here of the virtues of sour mash," the doctor intoned triumphantly and held up his glass. Anitra stared dubiously at the clear amber liquid.

"It's whiskey," Kirk said.

"Whiskey?" McCoy's honor was clearly wounded. "Bite your tongue. This here is George Dickel Old

No. 12 Brand, the finest beverage in the civilized galaxy."

"I see." She cocked a brow at the two of them. "And how many of these have you had?"

"Three," McCoy said.

"Four," Kirk corrected him.

She turned to the barmaid. "Four of those, please. Line 'em up."

"Er," said McCoy, "are you sure you want to do that?"

Anitra considered. "Yes. I took my medicine, if that's what you're getting at, so hopefully this poison won't eat another hole in my stomach. And it's going to be awfully boring talking to the two of you unless I catch up. There's nothing worse than being the only sober person in a crowd of drunks."

Kirk shot McCoy an amused look. The doctor shrugged. "Well, if you're going to do it, I suppose you may as well do it with the best."

"Where's Spock?" Kirk asked. "Did he give you a nice tour of the science academy?"

"He won't be joining us," said Anitra. "He went to see his parents again. And yes, the tour was very interesting. I've never seen anything like it. It's far better equipped than Star Fleet Academy."

"Better, maybe," allowed Kirk. "As to far better . . ."

"What made you decide to join us?" asked McCoy.

"It was Spock's idea, really."

"Spock's?!"

"Yes. He thought I should relax . . . have a little fun while I'm on shore leave."

Well, I'll be . . . , thought McCoy.

The barmaid reappeared. "Four shots of sour mash." She set them in a neat row in front of Anitra. "Pay up, please."

"Put it on my tab," Kirk said.

"Thank you." Anitra smiled at him genuinely and made a useless attempt to smooth her impossibly red, recalcitrant hair. "It's very kind of you after what I—"

"Don't mention it." There was a hint of ominousness in Kirk's answer. He was trying hard to maintain his anger at her, trying hard to dislike her, and failing at both.

McCoy made an unsuccessful attempt to stifle a giggle, and he finally let it out with helpless abandon until tears ran down his cheeks. "You really got us," he gasped at last. "Me, Spock, the captain . . ."

It was contagious. Kirk fought it at first, then succumbed graciously. Out of deference to the captain, she did not join in, but sat grinning at them both. Laughing, Kirk said to her, "Do it again, Ensign, and you're off my ship."

"Yes, *sir,*" she said softly. She tilted her head back and with a smooth flick of the wrist, poured down a shot. She set the empty glass down on the table with a click and proceeded to do the exact same thing with the second glass.

"You're going to get drunk," McCoy said, still weak from his outburst. At about that time, he became aware of a giant pair of legs standing next to him. They were attached to an equally massive body—the young man's neck was as wide as McCoy's waist. He wore the uniform of a maintenance crewman for one of the big cargo freighters, and above the left breast pocket was the inscription "Roy." He grinned down at Anitra with sandy-haired good looks.

"Care to join me at my table? You might have a little more fun with someone your own age."

In a second, Anitra became as cold as ice. She was really quite beautiful, thought McCoy, when she wore that haughty expression; it took away every trace of childishness and, with those high cheekbones, made her look exotic, almost feline. "My physician has advised me to stay away from cretins, thank you."

Roy blinked, unsure whether he had been accepted or rebuffed. Rather than leave quietly, he stood his ground (albeit swaying slightly) and began to speak in a loud, obnoxious manner, punctuating every third syllable by stabbing the air with his index finger in McCoy's general direction.

"What do you want to stay with them for? They're a little old for you, don't you think?" He peered unsteadily at McCoy. "Hell, *he's* almost old enough to be your father."

McCoy stood up, pathetically dwarfed by Roy's bulk.

"Sit down." Kirk tugged at his elbow.

"Not until the gentleman leaves." McCoy's eyes glittered angrily. "Get out of here and leave the lady alone."

"I am *not* a lady," Anitra protested, but she was ignored.

Roy giggled. "Are *you* going to make me, short-cake?"

"If I have to," McCoy said, realizing vaguely how very ridiculous he sounded.

Anitra stood up between them, annoyed with them

both. "I don't need any help from you, Doctor. And *you*," she turned to Roy, "get out of here before I make you regret it."

"Sit down," Kirk said, getting the uncomfortable feeling that he was helpless to avert certain disaster.

"I understand," Roy sneered at her. "Working your way up through the ranks?"

Kirk remembered hearing McCoy weakly exclaim "Oh, no" as the two of them watched Anitra launch a blow and follow it through to its subsequent arrival at its destination—Roy's stomach. McCoy, in an effort to be gallant, was in there swinging, but Kirk alone kept his senses. He alerted the transporter with no time to spare: as the three of them dematerialized, they had the satisfaction of seeing the Vulcan security guard intervene and drag Roy off, presumably to the local hoosegow.

The security code was no longer on, for the stone gate opened at Spock's touch. The sun was setting, and the interior of the house was dim in the twilight. Spock silently entered the long hallway, listening, but there was no sound, no sign of life in the large central room. The doors to the adjoining rooms had been shut.

There came a gentle thud behind him, and Spock whirled, his phaser drawn. A silver bird had hit the window overlooking the garden. After several seconds, it flew off, stunned. It would be best, Spock decided, to keep the phaser drawn, although he was no longer sure what effect a phaser stun would have on Sarek now.

He walked softly, too softly even for Vulcan ears,

and paused at each doorway, bracing himself to pull the trigger as soon as the door opened. There would be no margin for hesitation. But each door—Sarek's study, his parents' bedroom—opened on an empty, lifeless room.

And then he heard a muffled sound, like a sob, emerge from deep within the house from Amanda's library. He moved catlike toward the door, only to find that it had been locked from the outside, trapping whoever was inside. Even so, after he turned off the lock, he made certain to hold the phaser at chest level when the door opened.

For an instant, he did not recognize the wild-eyed woman, and would have fired the phaser had she not said his name.

"Spock." She gasped, trembling from relief and fear. Quite obviously, she had expected someone else. She flinched at the phaser aimed at her, and searched his eyes, her own almost wild, to be sure that this was indeed still her son.

Spock lowered the phaser, and Amanda rose from where she had crouched in the corner. She moved as if to embrace him, but controlled herself in time to simply gesture toward him.

"Spock—" she said and fought for air as if she had been running, "we've got to get out of here now. Your father—" Her face began to contort, and she tried to continue. "Your father—"

"—is not himself," Spock finished hoarsely, arguing with his guilt. "I know."

"You knew?" Her eyes widened, aghast and stricken, but did not accuse him; Spock was capable of doing that himself. He looked at the floor, wishing that she would curse him for it, knowing that she never would, and he reminded himself again of the logic that had dictated the necessity of this situation. At present, it appeared distinctly flawed.

He could not bring himself to answer her question, so he asked another. "Lieutenant Uhura said you called the ship looking for me. Why didn't you simply have them connect us? I was at the academy."

"He found me," she said simply and closed her eyes, "while I was trying to contact you. He realized that I knew. Silek . . . left a note for me, before he was killed." Spock looked away as her chin trembled. "It was your father who killed both Starnn and Silek." She covered her face with her hands.

"My father," Spock corrected her gently, "killed no one. Whatever, whoever controls Sarek now is responsible for their deaths." He gently pulled her hands from her face, and she tried to smile at him.

"He's coming back," she said, recovering herself. "He seemed to enjoy leaving me to think about my fate. I think he wanted me to feel terrified. I don't know where he's gone; I only know that when he comes back, he'll kill me. It isn't safe here. Please, please take me with you to the ship."

"Vulcan is infected with whatever destroyed the Hydrilla sector," Spock said levelly. "It isn't safe here for any of us."

Sanghoon Cho was alone in the garden lounge, feeding his Venus's-flytrap what looked to Tomson like raw ground meat. He peered at her with narrow, unfriendly eyes for a moment, blinked owlishly, and returned his attention to his pet.

"Someone said you were looking for me," he said. His eyes were still on the flytrap.

Tomson had been told that Cho was odd—he was indeed that and more. His face was Oriental, sharp and thin to the point of being gaunt, and it was framed by the most incongruous fluff of riotously curly brown hair.

And I have found you, Tomson thought. She said, "I have a few questions to ask you."

"Let me guess." A bit of meat dangled precariously from Cho's finger above the flytrap's gaping jaws; it fell, finally, onto the plant with a small slap. "Moh al-Baslama." He smiled ironically down at his pet as its jaws closed over its food. "Actually, it wasn't a guess. I have a very high *psi* rating."

"Well, you're right." She was unimpressed. "We have a warrant and my men are searching your quarters now."

"Let them search," Cho said mildly, looking up at last. "I didn't kill Moh. But I do have a question for you." He wiped his fingers delicately on a handkerchief.

Tomson waited.

"Just what the hell is going *on* on this ship?" He looked at her sharply as though expecting an answer; Tomson stood there, not saying anything. "People on this ship aren't the same anymore," he continued. "Something very weird is going on."

Tomson's eyes narrowed. Mentally, she saw herself confronting McCoy in sickbay and saying, *All right, Doctor, explain to me how this one slipped through the psychoscans*. To Cho, she said, "I don't know what you're talking about. Explain."

He knit his pale, oversized brows together and glanced suspiciously from side to side, as though fearful of eavesdroppers. "Moh was killed for noticing the changes in . . . certain people. He said too much to the wrong person. I sensed the changes in them, too— my *psi*, like I said. But after what happened to Moh, I thought it might be better to keep what I see to myself."

"If you want to do something for Moh, you won't keep it to yourself."

He looked up at her, and the fear in his eyes was unmistakable this time. "Look," he said in a tone far less contrived than the one he had been using with her, "something strange *is* going on. Check with Dr. Mc-Coy—he'll verify my sanity and my *psi* rating for you. I last saw Moh with one of his good friends, a guy from engineering—one of the ones who's changed." He shook his head. "Sometimes I think I'm the only normal one left in the department."

Don't bet on it, Tomson thought wryly. But she half believed him.

"Give me the name of Moh's friend," she said.

Cho leaned forward and whispered, "Stryker."

"First or last name?"

"Just Stryker. But don't go alone." He paused for effect. "You won't come back."

Tomson's mouth twitched. "If he's responsible for killing Moh, he's got more to worry about than I do."

Inside the ShanaiKahr Oasis, it was cool and dark. Outside, hot winds moaned ghoulishly.

"Hell of a place for shore leave," Stryker said. He had a clean, sincere face—handsome, but not so handsome that he had developed any conceit about it. "I spent a little time here once. You know what the Vulcans call that?" He thumbed at the small cyclones of red sand that beat against the door. "The word translates as 'breeze'."

Scott helped himself to his second round of Scotch. "I'd hate to see what they call a wind."

"You're right." Stryker grinned. "You would."

"What were you doing on Vulcan then?" asked Ensign Gooch. She was beautiful, dark and as tall as Scott, who sat most appreciatively next to her. "Serving time, Lieutenant?"

"Just a minute." Scott held up his hand. "I've been on shore leave less than an hour, and I've already heard more 'Lieutenants' and 'Lieutenant Commanders' than I care to. Enough of rank for the next few hours."

"A great idea, sir." Gooch smiled warmly at him. "Call me Mikki."

"There now," Scott said, "so it's Mikki, and Scotty and . . ."

"Stryker."

Satisfied, Scotty nodded at Mikki to continue.

She looked at Stryker with dark, innocent eyes. "I just wanted to know what penal colonies there were on Vulcan."

Stryker lifted an eyebrow in perfect native style. "I studied here for a year—exchange program."

"God help the Vulcans."

"It's true. Vulcan Science Academy, the engineering program." He leaned forward as if divulging a confidence. "Would you believe that Sanghoon Cho and I were in the same program together?"

"I can believe it," said Scott. "You're both excellent engineers."

"Thank you for the vote of confidence, Mr. Scott—Scotty." Stryker cast a smug look at Mikki.

She ignored it. "Now there's a queer duck. I'll agree that Cho is the best at what he does, but . . . he hardly fits into the Star Fleet mold."

"Not too well," Scott agreed.

"Cho always kept to himself a lot," Stryker said. "It was always hard to know what he was thinking about." He looked down at his beer. "He's gotten even stranger since Moh died."

Mikki's animation dimmed. "That was a horrible thing. And they've still no idea who—?"

Scott shook his head solemnly. "I've seen murders on starships before—of diplomats, spies and crew when aliens attacked or came on board—but I've never, in all my years in the service, heard of a crew member killed by one of their own."

"They say he was tortured," Mikki said softly.

Stryker stared morosely at his beer.

"He was a close friend of yours, wasn't he, Stryker?" Scott put a hand on his shoulder.

"As a matter of fact, he was." Stryker did not look up. "I don't suppose anyone would like to change the subject. I came here to relax."

Mikki brightened again. "I know—show Scotty your hypnotic trick. That's always good for a laugh."

"What's this?" Scott smiled tentatively.

The corner of Stryker's mouth crooked upward. "Okay, Scotty. Just look into my eyes and concentrate."

"Aah," scoffed Scotty. "I don't cater to that mumbo-jumbo stuff."

"It's not—whatever you called it. Come on, it's fun." Mikki glanced sideways at Stryker, her eyes shining. "I let him do it to me. Do I look any worse for it?"

Scott looked at her dubiously.

"If it makes you nervous, forget it," said Stryker. "But it's perfectly harmless."

"Well . . . all right," Scott said.

He looked into Stryker's clear, pale eyes.

For a moment, Scott had the sensation of being smothered, snuffed out. And then he was falling into the colorless eyes, becoming smaller and smaller. . . . The chief engineer's face showed a burst of unutterable horror, and then went completely slack as Stryker leaned across the table and touched his temples briefly. For a moment, Stryker's fingers glowed palely . . . and then he dropped his hands.

"See?" Mikki whispered. No one else in the crowded bar had taken notice. "I told you it would be fun."

Scott's face came alive again and smiled back at them malevolently.

Chapter Five

McCOY STOOD IN his office in sickbay. He'd treated his eye as soon as they'd made it back to the ship—miraculously, the others had escaped injury—and it was now only slightly swollen, although below there was a darkening semicircle. At the moment, however, Spock was far too distracted to notice.

"Physically, your mother is perfectly fine, with the exception of a few bruises, but she's pretty shaken up. I gave her a mild tranquilizer, and she's sleeping." McCoy nodded toward the inner exam room. "Now would you mind explaining what she's doing here?"

Spock looked from the captain to the doctor; both pairs of eyes were fastened unwaveringly upon him. He sighed and clasped his hands behind his back. "Perhaps now is the time for explanation. I regret I was unable to tell you earlier, but Dr. Lanter's safety was a paramount concern. Captain, the murder on board and the murders at my parents' house—"

"—are somehow connected," Kirk guessed.

He nodded. "So is the destruction of the Hydrilla sector."

"You're telling me that whatever killed the population of Hydrilla has spread?"

"It is spreading as we speak. It was brought back by the expedition crew, some of whom returned later on the *Enterprise*. Starnn was among those who returned to Vulcan earlier."

"You mean, the old man who killed himself at your parents' house?" McCoy asked.

"He was affected. But he did not kill himself."

"Wait a minute," said Kirk. "If he didn't kill himself, who did?"

Spock did not meet their eyes. "My father has been affected," he said tonelessly. "He almost killed my mother, but she managed to contact me in time."

The two humans looked at each other.

"Is there any way," asked Kirk, "that he can be—helped?"

"I do not know. The important question is whether Vulcan can avoid the same fate as Beekman's Planet. And not only Vulcan—the madness spreads quickly."

"The number of planets," Kirk said slowly, "that come into contact with Vulcan by cargo or passenger ships . . ."

"My God," McCoy interrupted. "How many shuttles run between Earth and Vulcan every day?"

"We must contact Star Fleet immediately," said Kirk.

"Star Fleet was already notified," Spock responded, "by my Uncle Silek before he left Hydrilla. Murders were occurring within the expedition even then. I do not believe security will be breached by any further explanation at this point. Dr. Lanter and I—"

"That damned project of yours," McCoy said, exasperated.

"You're telling me," Kirk's tone began evenly, but

rose with increasing anger, "that Star Fleet knew about this—knew of the danger—and let these . . . *things* on my ship? Exposed my entire crew, just like that?"

"Star Fleet does not inform me of the rationale behind its decisions," Spock answered calmly, "but I am sure the decision was not without justification. First, the *Enterprise*'s location made it a logical choice. And imagine the outcome, Captain, had Star Fleet sent a ship which was completely unaware of the danger. At least Dr. Lanter and I were able to warn you."

"It's not enough," Kirk said heavily. "Al-Baslama is dead. A man is dead. And now all of my crew is at risk."

"I regret his death deeply, Captain, and accept responsibility for it. But there was no way for us or Star Fleet to know that the researchers picked up by the *Enterprise* were affected. According to the information we had at the time, only Starnn and a few others who had returned to Vulcan earlier were affected. If anyone was remiss, it was I and not Star Fleet. Had I realized earlier what was happening on board—"

Kirk's expression remained grim, but he said, "If you were unable to figure out what was happening, Spock, then no one else could have. But what does all this have to do with Dr. Lanter and her safety?"

"Dr. Lanter is eminently qualified for this in a special way. She can sense the mental changes in an afflicted person."

"How?" asked McCoy. "I've seen her medical file. It states a normal *psi* function of around a hundred."

"For security purposes, her file lies, Doctor. Her *psi* function is well over five hundred."

Kirk whistled in surprise. "She can read minds easily. She knows if people have—changed."

"Yes. She was able to advise me of the change in my father. This makes her particularly useful to us, and unfortunately, useful to the . . . creatures."

"How so?" McCoy asked.

Kirk answered before Spock could. "If they had her telepathic abilities at their disposal—"

Spock nodded. "It would make them even more powerful than they are now. That is why Star Fleet insisted that as few people as possible be informed of our mission, and of Dr. Lanter's talent. If anyone who knew became affected—"

"She'd be the next target," Kirk finished.

McCoy frowned. "You never explained—if it isn't a disease, then what *is* it that we're talking about?"

"In the course of our investigation, we have come to believe it is not best described as an infection, but rather a type of mental parasite which takes control of the personality. It might be possible for several to infest one body. However, the change is not always noticeable; they seem at first to act very much the same as the original occupant."

"Parasite?" McCoy said in disgust. "Like a flea or a tapeworm?"

"Nothing so corporeal, Doctor. Pure energy, most likely. Dr. Lanter has suggested that they might be subatomic particles which can bond with chemicals in the brain. And apparently they thrive on sadism. Rather like—" He paused for a moment, hunting for the proper analogy. "You are familiar with Old Earth legends of demons?"

McCoy shuddered.

In the next room, Amanda's eyes were open.

"I wanted to let you know about the progress of the investigation," Tomson said. She sounded more up than usual.

"You have a suspect?"

"Yes, sir, a pretty good lead."

"Maybe I should congratulate you, Lieutenant. You haven't had much to go on."

She actually laughed at the other end of the intercom. "Congratulations would be premature at this point, Captain. I haven't made any arrests yet, and it's taken a long time to get to this point. I used the computer to eliminate those who were on duty, and verified the whereabouts of the rest by questioning. I've narrowed it down to one major suspect."

"Someone I know?"

"A Lieutenant Stryker in engineering, sir."

"One of ours," said Kirk softly. "And he came back from shore leave?"

"Records indicate that he has. I'll call you, Captain, if I scrape together enough proof to arrest him."

"You do that, Lieutenant."

Anitra was standing in the sonic shower when she heard the door to her cabin open. She waited for a moment for someone to call her name—Spock perhaps, in a matter of urgency when all civility must be thrust aside—but she did not sense him. In the next room was silence. She emerged from the cubicle and went into the outer cabin.

Spock's mother stood hesitantly by the door. She was extremely agitated, and her thoughts wove in and out so quickly that Anitra found it difficult to pick up their thread. Amanda glanced up at her and calmed her outward agitation, but the strong mental stream continued.

"You remember me, don't you?" She smiled sweetly at Anitra.

"Yes, of course." Anitra was too stunned for a moment by the incongruity of the situation to determine the proper course of action. Maybe the stress of what had happened to Amanda on Vulcan had induced some sort of breakdown, so that she walked unannounced into the rooms of relative strangers. Anitra stood just in the doorway to the outer area and moved no closer. *Spock, we need your help. . . .*

Amanda's eyes shone with an unnatural brightness. "I'm just sorry that the . . . circumstances on Vulcan prevented us from having the chance to really meet each other." She moved closer.

Instinctively, Anitra retreated slightly. There was something wrong, something terribly wrong. . . .

In midstride, Amanda seemed to double over. "Get away," she shrieked, "get AWAY." She crumpled to the floor.

A split second before she spoke, Anitra had already received the warning and was bolting past her to the door. She didn't make it.

Amanda rose from the floor in a smooth, graceful upsweep, as though levitated by some invisible force, and caught Anitra's wrists in a surprisingly firm grip.

All those years on Vulcan, with the higher gravity, Anitra thought with detachment.

"Look at me," Amanda snarled. "Look me in the eye."

"I know BETTER." Anitra freed her wrists from the hold and punctuated her statement by throwing the older woman against the wall. Amanda slid to the floor.

Anitra ran.

"Stop." The tone in which it was said was enough to make Anitra turn and see the phaser pointed at her.

"You can join us," Amanda said, "and you will be the most powerful among us. Or you can die here and now."

"Go ahead and shoot," said Anitra. She closed her eyes.

Behind her, the door to the cabin opened. Spock stood in the doorway, his phaser leveled at his mother.

Amanda's eyes rolled back in her head, and when the pupils reappeared again, the eyes were wide with terror. The voice that spoke was unquestionably Amanda's. "They say if you shoot me, even stun me, they'll kill me. I know you won't let them hurt me, Spock. I know that. I trust you." And she smiled at him, Amanda's sweet smile.

Spock fired.

Anitra was closer, but somehow Spock made it to his mother's side first.

Anitra threw an arm across her forehead and leaned against the wall. "I'm sorry it had to happen this way, Spock," she said softly. "Dear God, I'm sorry. Both of your parents now. I should have let you bring her here sooner. It's my fault."

Spock's shields were up, as they always were around her unless he was teaching the mind meld—partly out of politeness, to spare her from another's thoughts, but mostly, Anitra suspected, to protect himself. Now those shields were tight as a steel vise, with no trace of thought or feeling emanating from him now—but when he looked up at her, his eyes were haunted.

"She appears to be dead," Spock said.

Suicide, the forensics lab maintained even after Tomson had insisted on a second thorough investigation. Rodriguez had shown her the curly headed corpse himself, holding the knife with skillful precision. "See here," he pointed at the most gaping wound, "and here. You can see that it's a very awkward position from which to try and inflict a wound on someone else; I can't really thrust at that angle. But on myself—" He indicated exactly how the victim had inflicted the stab wounds upon himself.

Everyone in security and forensics was thus convinced that Sanghoon Cho had murdered Ensign Teresa Liu and turned the weapon on himself. They were quite hopeful that a thorough examination of Cho's quarters would yield enough evidence to credit him with al-Baslama's murder as well. Everyone, that is, with the notable exception of the chief of security. She was well aware that she could pin it on Cho if she wanted to, and make it stick, just as she was dead certain that Cho was not the man they were looking for. She knew who was, and she had absolutely zero proof.

Tomson was therefore not in a particularly good

mood when she went to question Stryker, especially because she had meant to bring someone with her—as a witness, she told herself, not because of the late Cho's caveat. But all of her people were tied up with the suicide/murder investigation, and she had no real excuse for questioning Stryker at this point anyway, since Cho's supposed suicide exonerated him.

The door to Stryker's cabin opened on the first buzz; Tomson had half hoped that it wouldn't open at all. She stepped inside, and as the door closed behind her, she felt a surge of panic. The outer office was completely dark; she could barely make out a male form in the room.

Stryker pressed the panel, and the lights came on. The man standing across from her could scarcely be described as threatening; he had an honest, friendly face, which at the moment wore a broad smile.

"Lieutenant Tomson," Tomson said stiffly. "I'm here to question you about the murder of Mohamed al-Baslama."

"Lieutenant Stryker," he said, still smiling, and held out a large hand which Tomson took reluctantly. His grip was warm and firm.

"I've been waiting for you," he said.

And then Tomson noticed his eyes—impossibly clear and colorless—and the sensation of being pulled downward, as if by an irresistible current. With sudden, heartsickening certainty, she recalled Cho's last words to her . . . and knew that he had been right.

In the next room, Amanda's body was gently illuminated by the pale blue glow of the monitor.

"She's on complete life support," McCoy said.

101

"Her condition is stable—" *If you can call it that*, he thought to himself. *My God, the woman was dead, pure and simple*. "—but it's going to deteriorate quickly unless something is done."

"How quickly?" asked Spock, as coolly as if he had just inquired about the weather.

McCoy hedged. "It varies with the individual, Spock. Two days . . . three, at the outside."

"And what do we do with everyone else who's affected?" Kirk asked quietly. "How do we stop it? Stun them all, and put them on life support?"

Spock remained silent, withdrawn. Anitra said, "That's what we haven't figured out yet, Captain. We're working on it."

"Is there any way we can protect ourselves—the crew?"

"Yes and no." Anitra sighed. "It appears to spread by some sort of contact with an infested person—and when I encountered Sarek after he was affected, I saw in his mind that he wanted me to look in his eyes; he was trying to focus them on me. I think it might be spread by a form of hypnosis. But I can think of only one sure-fire way to protect ourselves."

"Which is?"

"Getting off this ship."

The muscles in Kirk's jaw tightened. "I can't leave my crew at the mercy of these things."

"I understand your feeling, Captain," Spock said. He seemed distracted, as if he were looking at something very intently, though his eyes were not focused on anything. "But it is something we may have to consider. According to records found in Hydrilla, infestation occurs rapidly. Even more so once they have gained control of the *Enterprise*. Every planet within reach of this vessel could be affected."

Kirk did not reply.

"It seems to me," Spock continued slowly, "that if the creatures are capable of rational thought—and they do seem to be quite devious—they would want to attack the bridge crew first, and anyone who is knowledgeable about controlling this ship. From what we have seen, they are quite capable of using the abilities of those they have infested."

Kirk straightened suddenly and turned to McCoy. "Turn on the view screen."

"A hunch, Jim?" asked McCoy.

"Turn it on."

The darkness of the small view screen in McCoy's office melted away into stars.

Kirk's eyes held Spock's intently.

"Where's Vulcan?" McCoy asked.

Kirk was already signaling the bridge. Sulu answered; behind him, the bridge appeared normal, calm, unaffected. Kirk forced his facial muscles to relax.

"Status, Mr. Sulu?"

The helmsman smiled blandly. "Orbiting Vulcan as per your order, Captain."

The expression, the intonation, all of it was perfectly normal and right. "Who's got the con?" Kirk asked nonchalantly.

"Mr. Scott. Would you like to speak to him, sir?"

"Yes."

Montgomery Scott seemed as amiable as ever. "What can I do for ye, Captain?"

"What's our status, Scotty?"

"Just as Sulu said, sir. Still orbiting Vulcan."

"Scotty—" Kirk studied the face, searching for a clue, any kind of indication that would tell him not to continue, but found none. "Mr. Scott . . . we are *not* orbiting Vulcan."

The engineer almost chuckled. "I beg to differ with ye, sir—"

"Check your instruments. My view screen shows we're out of orbit."

"Sir—" a hint of a registered insult crept into Scott's voice "—I ran a diagnostics when I came on duty. With all due respect, Captain, if you're worried about the instruments, maybe you'd like to come to the bridge and see for yourself."

Anitra had been standing silently behind Kirk; he could barely hear her say the words, "Don't. Don't go to the bridge."

Kirk smiled down at his chief engineer. "Never mind, Scotty. If you say that the instruments are all right, I believe you. I guess I better have this viewer checked out. Kirk out." He turned to Anitra. "You're telling me that Scott . . ."

"I don't know for sure," she said. "I'm a touch telepath—I need the people in the same room with me usually, although some people transmit much more strongly than others. Call this a hunch, if you want, but do you really want to walk onto that bridge?"

Spock looked up from the nearest terminal. "Captain, I have accessed the navigational computers."

"And?"

"We are not in orbit around Vulcan. Our course heading is for the Rigel system."

"With billions of inhabitants," Anitra said.

"And Earth not far beyond." Kirk sat down heavily at McCoy's desk.

Spock faced him. "I suggest we take action to protect ourselves, Captain, and soon. Mr. Scott will no doubt have become suspicious, and it will not take him long to find us."

"We could barricade ourselves in auxiliary control," Kirk said, "but to leave the rest of the crew stranded—"

Spock was grave. "We can warn them from auxiliary control, Captain, tell them to lock themselves in their quarters, if necessary. But we cannot risk becoming infected ourselves. If we do—"

"Vulcan," Kirk said. "Rigel, Earth. But Scott's affected, and he knows this ship better than any of us. It won't take him long to break into auxiliary or find a way to override us."

"I respectfully suggest, sir, that the combined efforts of Dr. Lanter and myself just might prove to be a match for Mr. Scott's talents in that regard."

Kirk almost smiled and started to reply when the intercom whistled; for a moment, he did not answer.

"Ensign Nguyen from security, sir. There's been another murder—this one on B deck."

"Let me talk to Tomson," Kirk said.

"I haven't been able to raise her, sir, which is very unusual, since she's on duty. I'm extremely concerned about it."

There was a heartbeat of silence; Kirk looked grimly at the others as he spoke to Nguyen.

"Ensign, I want you to listen carefully. I am not insane, and what I am telling you is the truth. There are entities on board which have taken control of some of our personnel. They are spreading quickly, and right now we have no way of controlling them. These entities cause people to become extremely violent. I want you to go to your quarters and lock yourself in. Don't come out until you hear from me again. Do you understand?"

There was a startled silence at the other end of the intercom as Nguyen contemplated whether the captain was the victim of paranoid delusions . . . and then she replied meekly, "Yes, sir."

Kirk looked up at his friends. "It's time we headed for auxiliary control, gentlemen."

"Amanda," McCoy said suddenly.

Kirk stopped.

"We can't just leave her here," the doctor said. "God knows what they might do to her. The least of which would be to turn the life-support system off."

Spock closed his eyes and opened them again slowly.

"Any chance we can take her with us?" Kirk asked.

"I can rig up a portable life-support system—but it'll take a few minutes."

"We may not have a few minutes, Doctor."

"I won't leave her," McCoy said doggedly. He was aware of Spock's eyes upon him.

"Come with me," Kirk told the others. "McCoy, we'll meet you later in auxiliary."

"I . . . prefer to wait and escort the doctor," Spock said uncomfortably.

Kirk considered it and decided not to argue. "Dr. Lanter," he said, extending his arm in the direction of auxiliary control. She gave McCoy and Spock an anxious glance before she turned and left with him.

Chapter Six

"DOCTOR," SPOCK SAID, "I appreciate your concern for my mother's safety. But there is no reason for you to be detained any longer. If you will tell me where you keep your equipment, I—"

McCoy shrugged, uncomfortable at the Vulcan's remark; he far preferred argument as a means of communication. "Forget it, Spock. It would take longer to explain it than to do it. You stay here. I'll just be gone for a second." And he went into his office.

Spock turned his attention to the woman on the bed. The life-support system encasing her chest made her appear to breathe, made the pulse on the monitor beat steadily, made her seem alive, though the face was drained of color and already acquiring the pinched look of a corpse. Spock had to remind himself sternly that she was not alive.

Someone entered the room while Spock's eyes were on Amanda. He was about to compliment McCoy on his swiftness when he looked up and saw Engineer Scott. It took him no time to notice that Scott was wearing his phaser, while he was unarmed.

"Mr. Spock." Scott greeted him cordially. "I'm glad

to have found ye. There's something urgent we must discuss."

"I'm sure that it can wait, Engineer," Spock said evenly. He fastened his eyes on Amanda and kept them there.

"It's about the captain," Scott said.

"What about him?" Spock's tone was brusque.

"I wonder if you might look at me while I'm speaking to you, Mr. Spock. This is rather important."

"It *is* important," agreed Spock. "And that is exactly why I am not looking at you, Mr. Scott."

Scott appeared honestly puzzled. "I'm afraid I'm not followin' ye, sir. . . ."

Spock walked in measured steps halfway round the bed until he directly faced the door to McCoy's office. Scott followed, hoping to catch his gaze, and stood opposite him.

"I have nothing to explain to you," Spock said. "But there are some things you can explain to me."

"I'd be happy to, sir, but I'm not sure I understand—"

"For example, what has happened to her?" Spock nodded at the still form beneath the monitor.

"Now, why would I know anything about what happened to your mother, sir? Is she ill?"

"She's dead," Spock said, "and you killed her."

"Have ye gone daft, man, like everyone else on this ship? Begging your pardon, sir, but maybe you should pay a little visit to Dr. McCoy."

"Perhaps not you who control Scott, but one of you," Spock said.

Scott stared, thunderstruck, at him and put a nervous hand on his phaser. "Please, sir, I'll leave ye alone if ye'll just tell me where I can find the captain. There's been trouble on the bridge."

"What kind of trouble?" Spock continued to gaze steadily at Amanda. "I am second in command. Perhaps I can help."

"It's hard to explain, sir. . . . Ye'll have to come see it for yourself."

"If that is the case, then I cannot help you," Spock answered. "I will not leave this room."

He did not see Scott's face harden, did not see the cold hatred burn in his eyes, but he heard the shift in his voice. "Maybe you'll tell me where he is if you know it'll save your mother's life."

"She is already dead. You cannot harm her further."

"We did her no harm."

"We," Spock repeated softly. "How many of there are you?"

"Here?" The sound was hollow, thin, mocking. "Not so many yet. Look at me, Vulcan. Look or I will kill you."

"I am not as easily persuaded as some others. It would be wisest to kill me."

Scott raised the phaser, but a split second before he could fire, the heavy object in McCoy's hand impacted with his skull.

"A hypospray would have been somewhat less violent, Doctor," Spock chided. "I trust no permanent damage has been done."

McCoy bent over the unconscious engineer. "Poor Scotty. He'll have a hell of a headache when he wakes up." He frowned up at Spock. "You've got a lot of nerve, complaining about my methods. I just saved your life, Spock."

"And I am grateful, Doctor." He regarded the instrument in McCoy's hand with an arched brow. "The method was crude . . . but most effective."

McCoy grinned. "I never knew these portable life units were so versatile." He struggled with Scott's dead weight. "Come on. Help me get him onto an exam table."

"We haven't the time, Doctor—"

"Fine," McCoy gasped. "I'll do it myself. You take Amanda."

Spock sighed. He lifted the engineer out of the doctor's hands with enviable ease and laid him on the table.

Freed of his burden, McCoy leaned shakily against the table and turned on the monitor. "Looks like a headache is the worst problem he'll have. Okay, Spock, that's enough excitement for one day. Let's get your mother out of here."

"Doctor," Spock said, "the excitement has not yet begun."

Anitra stopped at the door to her cabin. "There are some instruments here I'll need," she said. "It'll only take a second."

"For what?" Kirk asked suspiciously. "More of your practical jokes?"

"Absolutely," she replied, her eyes dancing. "Only this time, I promise to play them on the opposition."

He almost smiled, then glanced warily about them;

the corridor was deserted. "You have exactly one second. And don't forget your phaser."

She hesitated in the doorway. "Us or them, is it?"

"Absolutely."

She set her jaw and disappeared inside. In less than ten seconds she was back with a phaser and a small kit. "Worried about me, aren't you?" She looked at him out of the corner of her eye.

"Lying about it would be useless."

She frowned, puzzled.

"I know about your *psi* rating, Ensign."

"Who told—" she began angrily, but he cut her off.

"After all, how else do you explain overhauling Scotty's engines . . . *exactly* as he would have? Lucky for you, wasn't it, that he was standing over you the whole time."

"I see." She turned red with a mixture of anger and embarrassment. "Well, maybe you don't know that Spock has been giving me lessons to shield out other people's thoughts. I am *not* a telepathic peeping Tom . . . *sir*."

"I'm sorry if I insulted you, Ensign. I suppose I'm rather ignorant about such things."

"I was just going to say," Anitra said haughtily, "that you can trust me in a pinch. I may be a practical joker, but I'm capable of being a team player."

"And if we're not in a pinch?" Kirk teased her gently.

"Then you can just forget it, Captain." And she smiled in spite of herself.

They managed to stop at Kirk's quarters as well for his phaser, then made it to their destination without incident. The door to auxiliary slid open, and Kirk caught a blur of movement as the young officer on duty quickly removed his feet from the console. He jumped to attention, blushing deeply.

Kirk smiled at him. "At ease, Ensign. Just a routine inspection."

The young man seemed confused. "Routine, sir? Are you sure we aren't on alert?"

"Why do you ask?" Kirk asked. Anitra stood behind him, her hand discreetly gripping her phaser.

"You're wearing a phaser, sir. Isn't that rather unusual?" He stared at Kirk, his eyes wide and innocent.

Kirk was debating whether or not there was time to explain, when suddenly he was overcome by a sickening dizziness and felt himself falling forward.

"No," shouted Anitra. He heard the phaser whine; somewhere, a body dropped to the floor.

Kirk drew in a breath and waited for his head to clear; behind him, Anitra dragged the young man out into the corridor and came back, locking the door behind her.

"Thank you," he said. "Is he dead?"

"Just stunned," Anitra said. "Amanda was apparently a special case."

The door buzzed.

"It's Spock," Anitra said confidently, turning off the lock. McCoy and Spock trooped in with Amanda in Spock's arms. A small device was strapped to her waist. Spock carried her as easily as if she were weightless and set her down gently in the small inner lounge area.

"You're late," Kirk said archly.

"I guess you could say we were held up," said McCoy. "It was Scotty, Jim. He was looking for you."

"Then it's a good thing Spock stayed to look after you."

Spock and McCoy exchanged glances. "I believe you're making an erroneous assumption, Captain," the Vulcan said.

McCoy beamed proudly. "Brained him myself with the medical equipment."

"How does the Hippocratic oath go, Doctor?" Spock asked rhetorically. "First, do no harm . . .?"

"Aren't we forgetting the fact that I also happened to have saved your life in the process?"

"Gentlemen," Kirk said and waved his hands, "there's no time for pleasantries. We've got to come up with some answers fast. It'll only take Scott a few hours to cut through the bulkhead and spring the lock."

"Indeed," Spock agreed. "Perhaps Dr. Lanter and I could attempt to slow Mr. Scott down somewhat." He looked questioningly at Anitra, who nodded. "The electrical energy of the lock itself might be used to generate a crude force field of sorts—"

"So much for the first problem," said Kirk. But we have a second pressing concern at the moment. We need a strategy for regaining control of this vessel."

"Simply accomplished," said Spock. "Neutralize the manual override and then channel the navigational computer through this terminal."

Kirk looked at the doctor. "How long do you think it will take for Scott to come to and start looking for us?"

"Not that long," McCoy said. "Probably somewhere between five and thirty minutes for him to regain consciousness. It wasn't that hard of a blow. And I'm sure his minions will be advised about us soon enough."

"And the next question is, once we have control of this vessel, what course heading do we take?"

McCoy shook his head. "Wherever we go, we'll spread these—whatever they are."

"Vulcan is already infested," Spock pointed out. "And shuttles run daily between Earth and Vulcan. It will spread, with or without the *Enterprise*'s assistance. I suggest we return there."

"Definitely," Anitra said. "But rather than risk spreading the problem, we should commandeer a shuttlecraft for ourselves and sabotage the ship so it drifts."

"But what's the point of returning to Vulcan?" Kirk wanted to know. "It's as dangerous there as it is on this ship."

"Even more so," Spock acknowledged gravely. "But our safety is not the object, Captain."

"Mr. Spock and I were commissioned by Star Fleet to investigate and find a solution for this problem." Anitra was suddenly all scientist. "In order to do that, we need an infected subject and the proper equipment for experimentation. And we need to be at a safe place where no one can locate us. Vulcan offers these things."

"But the chances of being infected or killed there—" Kirk began.

"Are high," Anitra conceded. "We don't deny that. But the academy has equipment that is far superior to anything we have here. And there's the hope that we can stop things before they spread to other planets."

"We have a subject here we could test—"

"Captain," Spock said quietly, "we need a living subject who is definitely infected. It is quite doubtful that my mother will be either one of those things."

"Vulcan is the only logical choice." Anitra's voice was calmly determined.

The ghost of a smile flitted over Kirk's face. "You're as bad as he is," he said with a nod at his first officer. "All right, then. If we're going to isolate them, then we'll need to cut off communications. I'll let the ensign do that from here, since she has already shown us her expertise in the matter. And we'll need someone to sabotage engineering so the ship will drift."

"I am qualified," said Spock.

"No contest, Mr. Spock. And I'll sabotage the sensors on the hangar deck."

"Hey," said McCoy, "what about me?"

"You can stay with me," Anitra piped up, "and provide moral support."

McCoy blushed; Spock looked nauseated.

"You heard the lady, Bones." Kirk winked at him. "I'm leaving. And once you're satisfied, you can keep Scotty from breaking in here, Spock, then you and the ensign can figure out how to make this ship drift short of blowing up engineering."

Kirk decided not to risk taking the turbolift down to the hangar deck; instead, he climbed down the emergency shafts connecting each level until it seemed his arms would fail. The corridor leading to the deck was, fortunately, empty—the area was not regularly patrolled. He had almost made it to his destination when he felt a giant hand clamped down on his shoulder. He reached instinctively for his phaser, but the hand pulled his arm and twisted it behind his back until the phaser clattered to the floor.

Kirk kicked backwards, freeing himself from the hold, and turned to face his attacker. The huge, beefy crewman wore the blood-spattered uniform of a maintenance technician and appeared to be in some sort of frenzy; he was snarling and his mouth was flecked with foam. Kirk froze and swallowed audibly.

The crewman roared and made a graceless lunge. Kirk sidestepped him neatly and glanced desperately about for the phaser. He spied it lying beneath the hangar console and scrabbled toward it, but the giant was not as slow-moving as Kirk had judged him to be. He pulled the captain toward him with a huge paw and laced his thick fingers around Kirk's throat. Red-faced, Kirk swung at his opponent, but the giant's arm was sufficiently long enough to hold Kirk too far away to do any damage. Kirk closed his eyes and was just pondering his next move when he heard a feminine voice say, "Don't hurt him, fool!"

The next thing he heard was the whine of a phaser. The force of it knocked them both to the floor. Apparently, the technician was stunned by the blast, for the footsteps Kirk heard approaching were those of a decidedly lighter person. He opened his eyes.

"Tomson." He smiled with relief. "Am I glad to see you."

"I'm glad I found you, Captain," she said in her typically flat tone and bent over him. "Are you all right?"

He sat up, waving away her attempt to help him up,

116

and fingered his throat lightly. "Thanks to you, yes."

"That idiot was really trying to throttle you. I couldn't let him do that. We need you."

Kirk was puzzled by the sudden warmth of her statement. "Where have you been, Lieutenant? Your people are looking for you."

"No kidding. What a coincidence." Kirk blinked and shook his head. Her eyes had always been small and narrow before; now they were huge, so huge they seemed to fill her face, fill the room. "We've been looking for *you*."

McCoy was pacing again. He had noticed the tendency twice already and had forced himself to sit down and relax, but was unsuccessful for more than five minutes at a stretch. It had been hours since they had first arrived in auxiliary. Spock and Anitra had rigged the lock, and after a relatively brief discussion with Anitra, the Vulcan had gone to sabotage the engines. He hadn't been gone all that long . . . nonetheless, McCoy found himself beginning to worry about the Vulcan. And as far as the captain was concerned, McCoy was convinced that something horrible had happened. "How much longer do you think it'll take 'em?"

"It depends," Anitra answered. "I've decided not to worry for another two hours. They might have to be patient and wait for people to leave before they can start working."

"And after two hours have passed?" McCoy asked gently.

Anitra sighed disconsolately. She was sitting with one elbow resting on the vast control console. Her chin was propped up on one fist, and her hair streamed, unruly, down her back. McCoy sincerely doubted that it had been brushed at all for the past few days. "Then we try to make it to the hangar deck, sabotage the sensors ourselves and take the shuttle-craft."

McCoy nodded unenthusiastically. "Makes sense. Do you think there's any danger of Scott finding us before Jim and Spock show up?"

"My God, aren't we dreary? Look, if it's any comfort to you, I haven't done anything to let them know we're in auxiliary control. The only thing I've interfered with is their internal sensors."

McCoy frowned at the realization that he was pacing again and sat down next to her. "Why would you need to do that?"

"They can't tell individual humans apart with an internal scan—but they could certainly find the only Vulcan on board. They'd have us in two minutes. I rigged it so they'll think it's an equipment failure. They'll never trace it here."

McCoy whistled in admiration. "You've thought of everything, haven't you?"

She struck a pose of mock arrogance. "My job, which, of course, I happen to be great at. Now let's talk about something more interesting. I'm sorry if I embarrassed you with my comment earlier."

"About my moral support." McCoy felt himself beginning to blush again. "Well, I'll have to learn to live with these things. Speaking about changing the subject, how did you ever come by a name like Anitra? I've heard of Anita—"

"That's usually what everyone hears the first time I

say it. Never listened to Grieg? The Peer Gynt Suite?"

"The song about the man going into the mountains, and he runs into all these little ghouls, and they dance frantically . . . that was a good one."

"That's The Hall of the Mountain King—an appropriate musical choice for the moment, eh? Haven't you heard Anitra's Dance?" And she hummed a few bars for him.

"Yes, of course. That's beautiful. Who was Anitra?"

"A houri."

"A what?"

"A seductress." She smiled appropriately. McCoy fingered his collar and cleared his throat until she laughed good-naturedly at him. "I'm sorry. I've embarrassed you again."

"Two to zero," he said. "No fair. Now I get to choose the subject."

"Fair enough."

"Why do you think you have an ulcer?"

Her smile faded until only a trace of it remained, and she looked down at the control panel in front of her. "I don't know. Stress of the job, I guess."

"With your sense of humor, I don't see how being a starship physicist would really get to you—especially since physics is your field. Most people who get to work in a field they love are perfectly content with their jobs."

She smoothed both hands over her forehead and scalp and grabbed the hair tightly at the nape of her neck, drawing it up as if the weight of it on her back had suddenly become too much. "That's true. Maybe the cause of my ulcer is something I'm not at liberty to talk about." Her head was tilted downward, toward McCoy, and her expression was now quite serious.

McCoy drew in his breath at how suddenly beautiful she had become. "My God," he said suddenly. "Your eyes are *purple*."

It caught her off guard, and she flushed scarlet to her hairline. "That's violet to you, Doctor."

"Whatever you call it, it's the prettiest color I've ever seen in a pair of eyes," McCoy said. "Embarrassed you, didn't I?"

"That's two for me, one for you."

"We haven't finished talking about your ulcer yet. And it just occurred to me that I ought to have a handicap—I'm at a disadvantage, since you know everything I think before I say it."

"There's an ugly rumor going around to that effect. Just please, don't blow my cover with anyone else. And, for the record, I've been taking lessons with Spock."

"What do you need lessons from Spock for?"

"So I can *not* read people's minds if I choose to. I was pretty miserable before he started tutoring me."

"So it wasn't just that mysterious 'project' all the time?"

"No. We've spent a lot of time learning to control my ability." She smiled ruefully. "If I hadn't learned about shielding, I think I would have finally gone crazy."

"I guess I never really thought much about it," said McCoy. "I always envied telepaths, being able to know what others were thinking. I guess it wouldn't be so much fun to constantly be flooded with everyone else's thoughts."

"There are times," she said with a wry expression, "when it isn't fun to know what others are thinking about you. It's kind of like finding out what someone has said behind your back. Sometimes even your friends might not think too much of something you do, but most people are too polite to come right out and say what they think. White lies are really more of a courtesy than you know. They really keep people's egos from constant bruising. I'm a great believer in white lies."

"And I believed you when you said I was cute."

She smiled the houri's smile again. "And you thought I was mooning over Spock."

"Now that's not fair," McCoy said. "You were reading my mind then."

"Tsk, tsk, Doctor—it was written all over you. You were certain I had joined the ranks of unrequited Vulcanophiles."

"Well," he protested half-heartedly, "you certainly had all the symptoms."

She twirled a lock of hair around her finger and studied it idly. "I suppose I do have a certain . . . fascination . . ." (McCoy winced at her use of the word) ". . . for all things Vulcan. Maybe it's because of the control they offer. After being at the mercy of everyone else's thoughts and feelings, not to mention my own, for so long, I guess I like the thought of finally being in control of it all."

"My dear, you are the last person in the entire world I could picture as a Vulcan. You're far too fun-loving for that. And if you cut yourself off from all that's human, you'll wind up missing an awful lot."

She laughed. "I suppose you're right."

121

"Of course I'm right. Just don't ask Spock to back me up."

"I wouldn't dream of it." She yawned and rubbed her eyes.

"A little tired?" he asked.

She nodded. "Another all-night brainstorm session with Spock."

"You're not a Vulcan, my dear. Just because you can compete with Spock intellectually doesn't mean you have to keep up with him physically."

"I know." She swiveled in the chair toward him and looked in his eyes intently. "But don't you think that the gravity of the situation merits the loss of a few nights' sleep?"

"God," he groaned. "Listen to you—you're even starting to *sound* like him. Look, we're not expecting anyone to come pounding on that door for at least an hour or so. Why don't you lie down for a few minutes?"

She looked painfully tempted. "I couldn't."

"Nonsense. You're the one running the show, and if you get too tired to think clearly, go stretch out in the other room and turn out the light."

"I suppose a few minutes wouldn't hurt," said Anitra. "But what if something happens?"

"I may not be a genius, but I think I can figure out if I need to call you. Go on, now."

She shrugged helplessly.

It was dark and cool in the little lounge. Amanda lay corpselike on the couch at the other end of the room, and while Anitra found it rather morbid sharing the room with her, there was no other alternative. She lay, as far away as possible, on the floor near the entrance.

Seconds after her eyes closed, Anitra was asleep, but it was not the pleasant experience she had anticipated. It was deep, trancelike, and she fell instantly into a nightmare.

In her dream, Anitra lay sleeping in the little lounge, through some nocturnal magic having acquired the ability to see through closed eyelids. Amanda was there, too, and rose silently from the couch—not using her legs and arms, but levitating straight up into the air. About five feet above the couch, she turned round and round, like a corkscrew, and then slowly righted herself, descending until at last her feet gently contacted the floor. Anitra struggled to scream McCoy's name, but the trance was too deep, and her vocal cords were paralyzed. Nor could she run, for her limbs had become too heavy to move. She lay perfectly motionless, except for her steady breathing, unable even to blink. The torment continued for some time— Amanda always nearing, always closer, yet never quite close enough to touch.

The touch of a warm hand broke the spell, and she woke gratefully, opening her eyes to darkness. "Doctor?"

"A neat trick, don't you think?" Amanda whispered slyly. Her eyes glowed palely in the darkness.

Chapter Seven

McCoy LET KIRK in the door to auxiliary control and closed and locked it as quickly as possible behind him.

"That was fast," McCoy said.

"That's why I get to be captain." Kirk looked around the room. "Spock's not back yet?"

"Not yet. Anitra wasn't expecting either one of you for another half hour."

"Where is she?"

McCoy lowered himself shakily into a chair. "We've had a little excitement while you were gone, Jim. Amanda—woke up."

"She did?" Kirk stiffened as though struck by a thunderbolt. "How is she?"

McCoy shook his head. "The things were playing possum on us, Jim."

"They did a damn good job."

"No kidding. My guess is they did it to get to Anitra, and they've been waiting for the opportunity all this time. I guess they found out about her somehow and really wanted her. That's my guess, anyway." He put his face in his hands and peered down through his fingers. "She went to lie down in the other room. Five minutes later, I heard her scream. Amanda was trying to strangle her."

"My God," Kirk whispered. "What'd you do?"

"You know me—never without a medikit. I gave that woman enough elenal to put her to sleep till next Christmas."

"How's Anitra?"

"Upset, naturally—other than that, just bruised. It gave her one hell of a scare. And she's exhausted from all that's been happening. Working late with Spock. She needed a rest. . . ."

"So you gave her a dose, too," Kirk sounded disapproving. "Not enough to keep her out until Christmas, I hope. We're going to have to be ready to leave as soon as Spock gets back."

"Nah," McCoy rubbed his face, "she'll be out another half hour, I figure. We can spare that much time, can't we?"

"Maybe," Kirk said. He started for the lounge.

"Jim?" McCoy called. "No point in going in there. They're both out cold."

Kirk stopped at the entrance to the little room and half turned his head back toward the doctor. McCoy could not see his face. "I just wanted to check on Anitra," he said easily. "No harm in that, is there?"

There was a heartbeat's pause. No harm that McCoy could see . . . yet there was something wrong with the question, with the way that Kirk stood in the doorway. McCoy realized that the hairs on his scalp and neck were standing straight up.

"Dear God," McCoy whispered. "Jim—"

Kirk's back relaxed. "Something wrong, Doctor?"

"Yes. Yes, there's something wrong," McCoy

croaked, forcing the words from his throat against their will. In the midst of his terror, he was suddenly struck by anger at what had been done to his friend. "Just what in hell *are* you?"

Without turning around, Kirk swiveled his head around at an impossible angle so that it faced McCoy.

"We," he corrected McCoy, smiling. "What in hell are *we?*"

Spock completed his task in engineering without incident, although he was considerably delayed by two engineering trainees engaged in a task near the matter/antimatter pods. He was making his way back down the corridor from engineering to the emergency shaft when he turned a corner and bumped directly into Lieutenant Uhura. Both of them did a double take, but Uhura had her phaser ready. Spock never had the chance to draw his. She waved it at him, looking bedraggled and a little wild-eyed.

"All right, stop it. Stop it right there or I'll fire."

He half raised his arms in acquiescence. From the intensity of her expression, she clearly meant business. Spock sighed. She was too far away for him to attempt to wrestle the phaser from her; logically, there was not much left to do, except to try to get closer to the phaser.

He took a tentative step toward her, but she would have none of it. "One more," she said, her voice deadly, "and I'll shoot."

"I have no doubt of that," Spock said and fastened his eyes on the deck.

She gestured menacingly with the phaser. "Where's the captain?"

Spock lowered his hands and said with mild exasperation, "That seems to be a most popular line of inquiry of late. Lieutenant, I'm afraid this will prove to be quite pointless. It would be less frustrating for both of us if you simply fired."

"*Get* those hands up," she barked with such explosive force that Spock raised his hands with exceptional dispatch. "And didn't your mother tell you it was rude not to look at people who were talking to you?"

Spock managed a step closer without her noticing. "Eye behavior is culturally bound, Lieutenant."

"You haven't answered my question."

Spock thought for a moment. "Yes, I believe she did."

Uhura grimaced as she thrust the phaser closer. "For God's sake, not *that* question—the one about Captain Kirk."

"If I knew where he was," Spock said, "I would not tell you. And at this moment I cannot say with certainty. I suggest you kill me and tell Mr. Scott that I knew nothing."

"Now why would I tell *Scott* . . ." Uhura's voice trailed off uncertainly.

At that moment, Spock moved close enough to see that the phaser was set on stun. In a breach of Vulcan ethics necessitated by the urgency of the situation, he lowered his mental shields just long enough to brush up against Uhura's mind. He looked up at her.

"Lieutenant Uhura," he said almost warmly.

"It *is* you, isn't it, sir?" Uhura grinned broadly, and for a moment was tempted to hug him. "Sorry, Mr. Spock. I should have known when you answered that question about your mother."

"Why were you so interested in the captain's whereabouts?"

"Who *wouldn't* be? Mutiny on the bridge, total chaos on the rest of the ship." She shuddered. "For a moment, I thought you were in cahoots with everyone else on the bridge—"

"Everyone else is affected?"

"On the bridge at least," she said soberly. "But not *me*. I had just reported for duty. When I stepped off the turbolift, I saw the stars on the view screen, and I was going to ask Mr. Scott if our orders had been changed." She closed her eyes and shuddered. "Sulu was sitting at his post. He looked like he was . . . hypnotized or something. He just sat, staring straight ahead, with his mouth open and Scott's hands were holding his head—sort of the way you do it, sir, for the Vulcan mind meld. But Scott's fingers . . . Mr. Spock, they were *glowing*. It seemed to travel down from Scott's hands to Sulu, because then Sulu's eyes started glowing with the same kind of light.

"I guess they heard me come in, because when they finished, everyone on the bridge was looking at me. They were all wearing these horrible, creepy smiles. . . . I figured I was their next target." She bowed her head. "You know, sir, I've never left my post before—"

"I know, Lieutenant. You had no choice."

"I didn't. I stepped right back onto the lift and went to my quarters and locked myself in. When I calmed down, it occurred to me that they might look for me there. Plus, I hoped if the captain weren't on the bridge, maybe he had somehow escaped, and maybe I could find him. That's when I ran into you." Her soft eyes widened. "Mr. Spock, what is *happening* to everyone?"

"You see that they are not themselves," Spock said quietly. "They are controlled by an outside force—some type of parasite. As you saw, they hypnotize their victims . . . and apparently need physical contact to complete the transference."

"Is the captain all right?"

Spock nodded. "As far as I know. But it is imperative that as few as possible know of his whereabouts."

"I understand, sir."

"We're going to have to leave the ship, Lieutenant. I regret that you cannot come with us."

She looked up at him, stricken.

"We're going someplace far more dangerous than the *Enterprise*. I cannot ask you to risk that. But you can return with me to auxiliary control. It's been rigged so that Scott and the others can't break in. You'll be safe there until we return."

"Thank you, Mr. Spock. Anything I can do to help—"

Spock paused. "I'm sure we'll think of something, Lieutenant."

There came the sounds of stirring and shadows moved in the inner room. *No,* McCoy screamed silently, mentally projecting with all his might. *Don't come out. Don't . . .*

But Anitra either did not perceive his message or did not care. She shuffled into the outer room, half staggering from the effects of the sedative, and leaned against the console heavily. Her hair was tangled, and she frowned at Kirk with the petulant expression of a child wakened from a deep sleep.

"Leave him alone," she said. "He's of no use to you. I'm the one you need."

Kirk's voice was gravelly. "If we need to take someone, we take her. If we don't need to take someone, we can still use him . . . for other purposes." He smiled menacingly at McCoy, who quickly lowered his eyes. "We don't just . . . leave him alone."

The door slid open behind him and Kirk turned. At the same time, Anitra fired behind him. Less than a second afterward, Spock fired from the doorway, and for an instant, the captain's body was suspended in the air, held upright by the sheer force of the opposing beams. The whine ceased and the body collapsed.

Uhura peeked tentatively around the door as both Spock and Anitra ran to Kirk's side; McCoy, stunned himself, took longer to get there.

"He'll be all right," Spock was saying by the time McCoy had his scanner out.

"How in God's name did you know to come?" McCoy marveled.

"A mental link," Spock said. "Dr. Lanter and I have found it to be invaluable. I only regret that I did not link with the captain as well. It would have warned me sooner of this."

"But the door was locked," McCoy said. "How the devil did you get in without buzzing us?"

Spock nodded at Anitra.

"Mental link again," she said. "I knew he was at the door. But I can't believe you didn't notice either. I thought I was so *obvious* at the console." She looked uncertainly over at Uhura, who had silently entered and stood looking down at Kirk.

"Lieutenant Uhura," Spock said, "will be remaining here."

McCoy smiled at her. "You don't know how good it is to see a friendly face again, Uhura."

She returned the smile. "You want to make a bet, Doctor? I'm just sorry about what's happened to the captain."

"We all are."

"It's time we got to the shuttlecraft," Spock said.

"Spock," McCoy began, "your mother—"

Spock straightened. "I cannot ask anyone else to take further responsibility for her. I'll sabotage the sensors while the two of you get to the shuttlecraft. I'll come back for her, but the instant you sense danger—"

"Spock," McCoy interrupted gently, "she came to."

Spock's eyes widened almost imperceptibly.

McCoy's tone was sympathetic. "They still have her, Spock. Somehow, they were able to control her bodily functions so that she appeared to be dead. That way she could get to Anitra without anyone suspecting. I've got her heavily sedated right now, but—"

Spock cut him off. "Then she stays on the *Enterprise.*"

McCoy watched his face intently for a shift in expression, but Spock was unflinching, steady. *So it's just that simple,* McCoy thought, but he could say nothing. Taking her with them now would be insanity; even he could not argue in favor of it.

Spock turned to Anitra. "The ship will begin to drift

shortly. I believe we'll have enough time before that happens to make it to the hangar deck. And we'll need to remove the captain and my mother from this room, for the lieutenant's sake."

"I'll take care of that," Uhura said. "You go on."

The excitement had gone a long way toward neutralizing the effects of the sedative; Anitra put her hands on her hips. "Well, what are we waiting for?"

Spock stopped in front of the circuitry panel near the entrance to the hangar deck. Anitra and McCoy hovered behind him, and he spoke to them over his shoulder. "Get into the shuttle and prepare for launch, but don't open the docking doors or move the craft until I've signaled that the sensors have been disengaged."

Anitra gave him a reluctant backward glance and headed for the hangar deck, where the *Galileo* stood ready for launch. McCoy did not follow, but planted himself firmly behind the Vulcan.

Spock frowned. "Go with Dr. Lanter, please. I can manage things here."

"I'll stay," McCoy insisted. "Maybe I can help."

Spock lifted a brow. "I seriously doubt it."

"I may not be much help as a technician, but I can serve as a lookout."

"I am perfectly capable of serving as my own lookout," Spock said, removing the first layer of paneling. "Interesting."

McCoy looked over the Vulcan's shoulder. "What's that?"

"This paneling has apparently been cut through before. Perhaps the captain completed his task—" He broke off suddenly and frowned.

"What is it, Spock?"

"The circuits have been polarized. It seems someone suspected we might attempt this and wanted to slow our escape. I'll have to recalibrate my instrument." He glanced back at the doctor. "This will take some time, Dr. McCoy. Please get on the shuttlecraft."

"If you can't cut the circuit in time, what's the point?"

Spock worked rapidly as he spoke. "You could attempt escape—"

"They'll blow the shuttlecraft to bits if they can track it."

"At least your chances would be better than if you remained on board," Spock said, exasperated. "I fail to see the logic of remaining here. You're providing me with no useful service—"

"I've got a phaser, dammit. I'm covering you."

Spock sighed and concentrated fully on the work at hand once it was quite clear that arguing would not change McCoy's mind. Despite his gloomy predictions, it took him no more than three full minutes to disengage the sensors.

"Good work, Spock," McCoy said approvingly.

"Good work, Spock," a rasping voice echoed. They turned to see Kirk behind them.

Spock made a subtle movement for his communicator, but Kirk's tightened grip on the phaser made him abandon the gesture. It would have been an altogether unnecessary one; the hangar doors parted slowly, and the three of them watched as the *Galileo* rose silently and sailed through the open portal.

Kirk found the nearest intercom and, without compromising his weapon's aim, hit the toggle with his fist. "Kirk to bridge. Lanter has the shuttlecraft—the sensors have been knocked out. Track her for now. I'm on my way."

He turned to his prisoners. "After you, gentlemen."

The bridge was eerie in the artificial evening's half light; the dimness left faces half in shadow. It was bad enough, thought McCoy, without the darkness. The faces of his friends wore expressions that were parodies of those the real owners would have worn.

Scott's eyes glittered palely as he rose from the con.

"View screen on," Kirk said and took his seat; for want of a better place, his prisoners stood alongside in their usual places, staring glassily ahead as the *Galileo* attempted to make its escape. "Helmsman. Approximate range."

"Three hundred kilometers, sir."

"Phasers ready," Kirk said.

"No," McCoy whispered urgently. Kirk swiveled in his chair to smile at him.

"Fire," he said, his eyes on McCoy. The doctor looked down, unable to bear what was happening on the screen.

"A direct hit," Sulu gloated.

McCoy looked sideways and caught a glimpse of Spock's face, illumined for an instant by the brilliant orange glow as the *Galileo* flared and burst into bits of wreckage, and then went dim again. Throughout, the Vulcan stared impassively ahead.

"What *are* you?" McCoy wheeled to face Kirk, his voice shaking with rage. "What kind of thing *are* you, that you could do that to someone like her—" He moved threateningly toward the captain.

Spock stepped in front of him before anyone else had a chance to stop him. "Doctor," he said softly, "there is no logic in making our situation any worse than it already is."

McCoy felt as though he were breaking into small pieces. *"Our* situation? Who gives a damn about our situation? You cold-hearted son of a bitch!" His voice rose until it cracked. "How could you just stand there and watch?"

Spock said nothing.

"How could you!" McCoy spat vehemently, but the Vulcan remained silent.

"Gentlemen," Kirk's tone was mocking, "she had it easy. You, on the other hand, will not." He nodded at Scott. "Mr. Scott, escort these prisoners to the brig." He leered at them. "I want you to think—really *think* about what happened to people on this ship who were . . . uncooperative."

"Such as al-Baslama," said Spock coldly, "and Liu . . ."

The remark seemed to please rather than anger him. "To mention only two. We don't need you, gentlemen. But we can use you . . . at our leisure, and for our own pleasure."

His chilling smile was the last thing McCoy saw as they left the bridge.

* * *

McCoy had not actually seen the shuttlecraft be destroyed, but he had seen the glow of the flames on Spock's face, could even now see the death scene played back in Spock's eyes—the metal hull ripped, twisted, hurtling in a thousand directions as the initial burst of flame was extinguished rapidly in the oxygen-less reaches of space. Spock sat on the floor of the brig, his back straight against the wall, morose, untouchable. McCoy sat in the opposite corner. From where he was, he could just see the guard's back on the other side of the force field.

McCoy was hurting too badly at the moment to keep his feelings to himself any longer. He thought of Anitra, so beautiful, so . . . *alive*—and found himself trying not to weep in front of Spock. He surreptitiously wiped his eyes on the corner of his sleeve.

"How long do you think we have?" he asked when he could speak again.

"Impossible to estimate." Spock's voice had no inflection; his eyes were focused on a far-distant point.

"I wasn't really asking for an estimate," McCoy said in his best conciliatory manner. "I guess . . . I was just trying to make conversation."

As soon as he said it, it struck him as a stupid thing to say; Spock, of course, would be in no mood for idle conversation. He sat, a wooden Vulcan deity, showing no signs of having heard. There was probably no logical reply, McCoy guessed, to such a statement.

He came to the point. "Dammit, Spock, I was trying to apologize for what I said on the bridge."

"I have come to expect such outbursts, Doctor."

"It's just that . . . she's dead." McCoy blinked

rapidly at the sound of the words. "How can you not react to that?"

Spock's eyes were on him, and so cold that they seemed to burn right through him. "I need not account for my behavior to you."

"You're right," McCoy sighed.

It took Spock a full minute to register what he had just heard. He turned to McCoy, both eyebrows raised in an expression of honest amazement. "That is the first time," he said slowly, "that you have ever said those words to me."

McCoy said nothing.

"Your normal reaction at this point is to argue even more strenuously."

McCoy shook his head and rested his chin on his knees. "What's the point? They're going to torture us . . . then kill us, if we're lucky."

Spock nodded in somber agreement.

"Why make it any worse for you? It wasn't anyone's fault. We're both sorry she's dead. It's just that I . . ." McCoy broke off.

"You are . . . fond of her," Spock said gently, almost kindly.

"I didn't think you were one to notice that sort of thing," McCoy said, blinking rapidly. There was no longer any reason not to admit it—there would be no further arguments where Spock could use such knowledge as ammunition.

"You give me little credit, Doctor," Spock said in the same soft tone. It was one that McCoy had not heard before—Spock with his defenses down. "I've been observing humans for many years now. It's a phenomenon I've had the opportunity to see numerous times. How else would you explain your reaction on Vulcan when you saw me emerge from her bedroom?"

"It's just a damn shame—all of it." McCoy was beginning to feel downright tearful. "We were so close to succeeding, and she was our only hope. I wish now I had gone on that shuttlecraft with her."

"There's still a chance," Spock said softly. He seemed to be studying the doctor with a curious look of pity.

"What chance?" McCoy laughed hollowly. "It's all over, Spock. They've got Jim, they've got the ship and probably most of Vulcan by now. Anitra was Star Fleet's great hope and now . . ."

He looked over at Spock, but the Vulcan was no longer listening to him—he was looking over at the door to the brig, where the security guard lay sprawled on the floor. There was a small crackle as the force field in front of them melted away.

McCoy looked up and grinned so hard it hurt.

"Just sitting around doing nothing?" Anitra teased. "Come on." McCoy made a move to hug her, but she sidestepped it and thrust him forward. "There isn't time. The hangar deck."

"She's alive," McCoy said, beaming stupidly and moving it.

"Obviously," Spock said, and for a moment McCoy feared the Vulcan might actually smile.

"Wait a minute. Now wait just a minute!" Outrage crept into McCoy's voice, and he vacillated between the ridiculous urge to kiss the Vulcan or kill him. "You knew. Damn you, you pointy-eared bastard, you *knew*."

"Dr. McCoy, I have tolerated enough remarks concerning my legitimacy for one day—"

McCoy laughed. "She's alive."

"Not for long, if you don't shut up," Anitra said, feigning irritation, but nonetheless pleased by McCoy's reception.

"But how—?"

"I put *Galileo* on autopilot and hoped they'd assume I was on it. The sensors are still out on the hangar deck, and I've got another shuttlecraft all set up to go."

"Then let's get the hell out of here," McCoy said and grinned.

Chapter Eight

McCoy STEPPED OUT into the Vulcan night. Above him the sky dazzled with an alien configuration of stars, brighter for the absence of clouds and moons. He tried to orient himself, but the myriad stars made it impossible. A dry, chilling breeze swept the sand, and McCoy shivered and rubbed his upper arms briskly. The nearest large body of water lay more than a thousand kilometers to the south; without the insulating properties of water or clouds, the desert surrendered its heat quickly. He took a step forward and half stumbled; in spite of the brilliance of the stars, his eyes were unaccustomed to the darkness.

"Roughly five-point-six hours before dawn." Spock emerged from the shuttlecraft behind him. "We should be able to reach the capital before that, if we maintain a good pace."

"Why the urgency?" McCoy asked. "You aren't expecting anyone to be looking for us, are you?"

"Doubtful," Spock said. "With communications on the *Enterprise* sabotaged, there is no way for anyone on Vulcan to know we're here. But I do not believe you would enjoy crossing the desert during the day."

"I won't argue that with you, but I still don't see why we have to hike five hours through the desert."

Spock sighed. "As I explained to you before, Doctor, secrecy is essential. The closer we land to a civilized area, the greater the risk of detection."

Anitra poked her head out the door and wrinkled her nose. "Chilly out here," she said. "Any chance this craft is equipped with some thermal suits?"

"Check the storage area in the back," McCoy suggested. "Of course, I don't know how recently the ship was stocked. No one was expecting to be taking it anywhere."

She came out a moment later carrying two thermal blankets and handed them to Spock. "This is all I could find."

"Not the most elegant means of dealing with the cold," Spock said, eyeing them, "but suitable." He handed one each to McCoy and Anitra.

"Just a minute," Anitra said, "what about you?"

"I am better equipped—"

"You're forgetting something . . . sir," she interrupted, tacking on the "sir" as if the protocol of rank were an extreme irritation best forgotten. "Females are far better equipped than males to handle cold."

"You're forgetting one important thing," Spock said stiffly. "I am a Vulcan. And more importantly, I am the ranking officer here; therefore, I make the decisions."

Anitra blushed and closed her mouth; without a word, she pulled the silver blanket tightly about her shoulders. It was all McCoy could do not to express delight at her success in insulting Spock, but he said nothing and put the blanket around his shoulders.

"I'll go first," Spock continued, "as my night vision is better and I am most familiar with the hazards of the desert." He and McCoy both watched Anitra to see if she would also take issue with that statement; McCoy felt almost disappointed when she remained silent.

The sand was soft and yielding, and the wind whispered it across the tops of their boots. McCoy could not see where his feet were falling, and found it a struggle just to keep pace behind Spock and Anitra. In the distance, he heard a rasping, metallic scream, and shivered.

"What the hell was *that?*"

"A *le matya.*" Spock turned his head so that the wind would not carry his words away. "There is no cause for alarm. From the location of its scream, I would say that we are downwind of it."

"Oh, great." McCoy's eyes widened and searched dubiously about, but saw nothing but stars and darkness. After an hour, when no attack was forthcoming, he gave himself completely to the task of keeping up. They continued in this way for at least an hour, by which time McCoy was huffing, while Anitra and Spock seemed quite unaffected.

"I don't suppose," McCoy called over the wind and the rumbling of his stomach, "that anyone thought to bring anything to eat?"

Spock looked at him, but did not deign to reply.

A sudden, sharp force lashed itself about McCoy's lower leg and ankle, yanking him to the ground with such force that he emitted a short, soft yelp. It pulled him backward with numbing speed, and he slid on his stomach, cursing and sputtering sand, his fingers leaving a trail of furrows across the desert. The blanket was left far behind.

McCoy was far too stunned to wonder what was happening to him; caught up in the preoccupation of keeping his face out of the sand, he scarcely registered the lightning glow of a phaser nearby. With a sudden jolt, the pulling stopped. Gingerly, he raised himself to a sitting position and examined the thick dark green vine spun tightly around his ankle. Spock knelt next to him and gently began to unwind it.

"What in God's name—" McCoy began shakily.

"A *d'mallu* vine, Doctor." Spock held up the three-foot length for McCoy to inspect. "You're quite lucky I was watching when it attacked. Otherwise, it would probably have been some time before we missed you."

"Thanks a lot," McCoy muttered.

"Had you been dragged another few yards—"

"You should have seen it," Anitra volunteered enthusiastically. "It had this huge, gaping mouth—"

McCoy shuddered. "Don't tell me. I don't want to know."

"Actually, this attack comes at a most convenient time," Spock said. "Didn't you just say you were hungry?" He broke off a piece of the vine and proffered it to McCoy, ignoring the doctor's thunderstruck expression.

McCoy paled. "Oh, no, now wait a minute." He held up his hands to ward off the thing. "That thing just tried to eat me. I've heard of getting even, but this is just too much."

The Vulcan bit into the refused morsel with a loud

143

crunch and began chewing with a decidedly whimsical expression.

"Spock, I'm surprised at you. You're supposed to be a vegetarian."

"It is a plant," Spock replied serenely. "Surely you aren't that squeamish, Dr. McCoy. I have seen you eat things capable of far more movement than a d'mallu."

He snapped off another piece of the vine, not without a glimmer of amusement, and handed it to McCoy. This time, logic and hunger won out, and McCoy took it, though reluctantly. He bit into it and found that it had very little taste—crunchy and slightly sweet. He began to eat with more relish, and with a rather smug sensation of revenge.

"Can you stand, Doctor?" Spock asked.

"Of course." McCoy scrambled to his feet—and had to bite his lip to keep from swearing. The d'mallu had lost the battle, but it had managed to inflict a few wounds: the ankle was badly bruised. McCoy wobbled, struggling to maintain his balance in the soft sand, and smiled insincerely. "Just shook me up a bit, that's all."

"You're a terrible actor," Anitra said.

"You shouldn't walk on it," Spock said. "I can carry you without any appreciable loss of time."

"Like hell you will." To prove his point, McCoy began walking briskly ahead.

Spock sighed. "That's all very well, Doctor. But ShanaiKahr lies *that* way." He pointed in the opposite direction.

The sun rose at last, heating the air with alarming efficiency. Anitra and McCoy had shed their blankets almost at the first rays of sunrise. According to Spock, they were still two hours from the outskirts of the capital; because of McCoy's dogged insistence upon walking unaided, they had made little progress during the night. Spock had at first kept up his rapid pace, only to realize that McCoy was being left behind. And McCoy's vehement refusal to be carried made it clear to Spock that invoking command privilege in this instance would be futile; the doctor obviously found the idea of court-martial preferable to that of being carried by the Vulcan.

Eridani climbed quickly in the sky and brought with it heat and blinding brightness. McCoy had been unable to see the night before for the darkness; now he could not see for the light. Spock turned to him, concerned. "It's quite dangerous even for a Vulcan to stay long on the desert, unprotected as we are from the heat. I suggest we alter our course and head for shelter until evening."

"Shelter?" McCoy squinted about uncertainly. The desert stretched to infinity in all directions. He raised his hand to his forehead to wipe away a bead of sweat, but the dry heat had already evaporated it and he touched dry, hot skin. His ankle was throbbing now to the point that he no longer pretended it was not painful.

Spock studied his two companions. Anitra appeared to be in fair shape; being young and female, she suffered from the heat far less than did the doctor. She had walked uncomplaining the night before, with silent determination. But Spock was definitely worried about McCoy. Exhausted from the previous evening's trek, McCoy was shuffling at an ever-slower pace, and the heat had already turned his face pale gray. He also desperately needed to stop and rest his ankle—but Spock knew that to lie down in the desert sun was the sheerest form of idiocy.

"There is shelter," Spock said. "Forty minutes in that direction."

"Forty minutes?" McCoy rubbed his face wearily. "Why not just go the two hours? At least we won't have to backtrack."

"Every minute spent in the sun," Spock said, "is a minute closer to death." For humans, at least, that was true. Even a Vulcan equipped with a desert soft-suit and an ample supply of water would think twice about a two-hour hike at midday.

"Whatever." McCoy was too weak to argue. Anitra and Spock stopped and eyed him with concern as he slowly trudged forward. "Well, come on," he said irritably, looking back over his shoulder at them. "Every minute in the sun . . ."

Anitra and Spock followed, but this time they walked on either side of the doctor.

That way, when he collapsed twenty minutes later, they were easily able to catch him.

Anitra lowered herself into the steaming water smoothly, slicing it without a splash. After the heat of the desert, she was surprised at how the hot water refreshed her. She sank down until it covered her head, fanning her hair out behind her. The long copper strands floated lazily to the surface. She was buoyant, so that she had to paddle to stay beneath the water's surface, which smelled and tasted strongly, but not unpleasantly, of mineral salts.

She opened her eyes and looked down into darkness: except for the shallow rock shelf near the shore, the pool was bottomless, so that from a short distance away, the water appeared black. She let herself drift back up to the surface, her hair clinging, soaked, to her scalp, and began to swim.

After the past night's journey, it did not take her long to exhaust herself. She closed her eyes and floated. The water supported her softly, and she sighed as she attempted to forget the horror of the past few days.

She had almost succeeded when something brushed, squirming, against her arm. Startled, she pulled out of the float. A small water beetle was skimming the surface of the water next to her; on the other side of the pool, hundreds of beetles skated in a graceful aquatic ballet. She pushed the water with a cupped hand and sent the insect riding a small crest of wave toward its peers.

She floated again, this time with her eyes open. A hundred feet above her, the ceiling of the great cavern hung with a thousand razor-sharp stalactites, which seemed in imminent danger of falling, like a sword of Damocles, upon the heads of whatever innocent swimmers happened to be in the pool. No doubt they had appeared that way for millennia, but Anitra chuckled silently at the irony—to come this far, only to be done in by a stalactite—and amused herself by calculating the odds.

The immense silence of the cavern magnified sound, so that she started at the sound of footsteps ringing against the hard stone floor. With a downward-circling motion of her arms, she righted herself gracefully in the water. Spock had been so concerned with McCoy in the small cave that she had expected to bathe in the spring with complete privacy. She lowered herself in the clear water in a useless gesture of modesty until it reached her collarbone.

The footsteps stopped at the edge of the pool, and Anitra started. A young Vulcan male, perhaps seventeen or eighteen years old, knelt at the edge, dressed in an ankle-length robe that made him look like a monk. His striking features were perfectly composed, but his eyes were wide.

"Who are you?" he asked in Vulcan. His voice was surprisingly deep.

Anitra stammered for a moment, trying to remember the few words she had learned in Vulcan, failing entirely. "I don't speak Vulcan," she said, feeling the warmth rush to her face. She folded her arms strategically in front of her.

"I am Soltar," the Vulcan said in English. "Who are you?"

"Anitra." She was sorry as soon as she said it; after the paranoia of the past few days, she feared leaving a trail that anyone from the *Enterprise* could follow, but she had sensed no evil in the young man, and there was no reason to mistrust him. She came closer to the edge of the pool so that the rock at the edge would at least partially hide her from Soltar's gaze.

"It is a very unusual name," he said. "Is it Terran?"

"Yes," she said. There was no point in lying about anything else.

"How have you come to be here? Terrans do not come to Gol."

"I might ask you the same thing," she said, and

Soltar digested the remark, wondering if it were meant to be taken literally.

He was rescued from his dilemma by Spock, who emerged from the cave in the rock wall, where he had been treating McCoy. He spoke to the young Vulcan, and Anitra watched his manner change, become stiffer, more formal, his face as masklike as Soltar's. He stood on the opposite edge of the pool from Soltar, while Anitra stayed in the water between the two, more than a bit uncomfortable at being naked in the water while the Vulcans conversed, apparently quite oblivious to her discomfort.

"I am Spock," he said. "We require assistance. Our other companion is in there—" he nodded toward the cave "—a human, who suffers from the heat."

"I will take you to the High Master," said Soltar.

"I don't suppose I could dress first," Anitra said. The Vulcans looked down at her, startled.

Soltar led them down a perfectly symmetrical staircase which had been carved into the rock. Spock and Anitra followed at a distance that allowed for some privacy of conversation.

"Amazing," Anitra said at the sight of the stairs.

"The mountains of Gol have been inhabited for thousands of years by the masters," Spock said.

"The masters?"

"The ones who practice Kohlinahr, the perfect mastery of emotion, and instruct others as to its attainment. From his robe, I would say our guide is a postulant—new to the order. He has not yet attained mastery."

"Seems close enough to me." She lowered her voice

even further. "Spock—I told him my name. Do you think it might be dangerous?"

Spock shrugged. "It would be nearly impossible for anyone to trace us here. And the masters lead a life completely isolated from civilization. They generally accept one postulant a season, so I doubt that we need worry about contamination here."

Anitra sighed. "That's a relief. How's McCoy?"

Spock looked over at her. She had asked the question casually enough, but even now, she could not hide the eagerness in her eyes. "He seems to have suffered no permanent damage."

"I'm glad," she said simply and looked away.

Spock did not answer.

Soltar came to a halt in front of a high stone door and pushed it aside; inside, the High Master sat, regal and silver-haired, in the solitude of an empty chamber.

"High Master T'Sai," Soltar said from a respectful distance.

She opened her eyes and looked at him.

"Strangers," said Soltar, "needing our assistance." He bowed and left the room.

T'Sai's face was quintessentially Vulcan: expressionless, devoid of emotion, ancient and ageless at the same time. Yet it lacked the severity of most Vulcan countenances, and the masklike quality of Soltar's or Spock's. It was benign, childlike, a sincere reflection of her innermost being. Although the others struggled to suppress emotion, T'Sai had simply emptied herself of it.

Spock stepped forward. "I am Spock."

"Spock," T'Sai repeated in a very low, dreamlike

voice. "I have heard the name. The child of Sarek and Amanda, is it?"

Spock bowed his head in acknowledgment.

"What manner of assistance do you require of us, Spock?"

"There are three of us," Spock said. "We were crossing the desert at night when one of us—a human—was injured, slowing our pace. When sunrise came, the heat was too much for him."

"We will see to him," T'Sai said. "What more can we do?"

"We need food."

"That can be provided." She examined him with serene black eyes. "You are wearing communicators—the Star Fleet uniforms. Why did you not contact your vessel for assistance?" There was no suspicion in her question; merely—or perhaps Anitra imagined it—the smallest hint of curiosity.

"Our ship is out of range. There was no other means of assistance."

"The frequency on your communicator could have been adjusted to contact authorities in the capital."

Spock bowed his head silently for a moment. When he raised it, he said, "We do not wish to have the authorities aware of our presence. Here, in the isolation of Gol, you are not aware that an evil has invaded our people."

Anitra watched, but T'Sai's expression shifted not even minutely. "What evil is this?"

"An evil which devours personalities. It . . . possesses. It brings about violence. Vulcans are murdering each other, T'Sai."

T'Sai's eyes closed. "As in the time before Surak." She opened them again and fastened them on Spock. "This evil—how many are affected?"

"Impossible to estimate at present. It spreads rapidly; it is the same force which destroyed the Hydrilla sector. You must maintain your isolation; you must not accept any new postulants."

"But what of Vulcan?" T'Sai asked; her voice was as soft as a sigh. "Shall we remain in the mountains while madness spreads?"

"We're going to the capital to try to reverse what has happened," Anitra spoke up. From the silence that followed and the look that Spock gave her, she realized that she had committed a breach of Vulcan courtesy.

"And you are?" T'Sai asked.

"Anitra." In spite of herself, she flushed.

"I am not familiar with the name. It is Terran?"

"It is."

"It is imperative that we reach the capital, T'Sai." Spock gestured toward Anitra. "My companion here has an uncommon telepathic gift; she is able to discern the presence of the evil force. She is also a scientist of great capabilities. With equipment at the Vulcan Science Academy, we hope to find a means of rescuing our people."

"She would benefit from our training," T'Sai said approvingly. "And the human with you?"

"A physician. When our ship was overtaken, he was one of the few who escaped control."

"If you reach ShanaiKahr," T'Sai said slowly, "but find yourselves unable to locate a solution—what then?"

"Vulcan will suffer the same fate as the other planets in the Hydrilla sector. And not only Vulcan will be affected. The planets in the Hydrilla sector had developed only a very crude means of interplanetary travel; they had not yet discovered warp drive and could not leave their own solar system. With starships available to carry the madness—"

T'Sai raised a hand to silence him. "You speak of the destruction of the galaxy," she said.

Chapter Nine

"FEELING BETTER?" ANITRA knelt down next to Mc-Coy and smiled at him.

He opened his eyes and smiled at the sound of her voice and struggled to sit up. She put a hand on his arm to help him; he tried to push it away, but she was firm. "If you aren't a sight for sore eyes . . ." He stretched stiffly.

"I don't suppose those rocks make a very comfortable bed."

"Beats the desert all to hell." McCoy unconsciously rubbed the bruised ankle, keeping his eyes on her all the while, mesmerized. She had changed out of her uniform and wore the soft, draping folds of a desert softsuit—a size too large, but its golden color made her hair seem, if at all possible, even redder.

She was meeting his eyes intently, the imp replaced by the houri. "You had us very worried."

"Sorry about that. You'd never know it, but I once got a merit badge in hiking—"

"A what?"

"A merit badge. Weren't you ever a scout?" McCoy asked.

She shook her head.

"Pity. You'd have made a good one."

"Thanks . . . I think. Hungry?"

McCoy shrugged. The nausea, at least, had passed. "A little. But if all you've got is d'mallu vine, you can forget it."

Anitra laughed. "Nothing of the sort. I can bring you a home-cooked meal—vegetarian, of course, but not bad."

"Where did you find something to cook in all this sand?"

"There's a group of about fifty Vulcans living in this mountain. Spock calls them the masters of Gol. I think it's some sort of religious thing. They keep to themselves—they didn't even know what's been happening on Vulcan."

McCoy made a face. "Religious Vulcans, huh? I bet they have one hell of a sense of humor."

"Not particularly. The High Master had the nerve to tell me I should sign up for Vulcan lessons."

Her expression of outrage was so comical that McCoy laughed. "I can just see it now. What'd you do, put a frog in his ceremonial robe?"

"*Her* robe," Anitra corrected. A look of mischief crossed her face. "Frogs are few and far between here, but it's an idea. . . ."

"Oh, no," McCoy said with mock horror, "let's not get you started—"

"Don't worry," she sighed. "Spock would never forgive me."

"So? All the more reason to do it. Besides, what do you care what Spock thinks? Anyone who would risk court-martial playing a joke like that on the captain—"

"Maybe that was the idea," she said, but she still smiled.

"Uh-oh. This sounds serious."

"I'm never serious. It's just that I hate spit and polish, the whole rank thing. There are days when I'm sorry I signed up."

"Why did you?" McCoy asked seriously.

"It seemed like fun. Travel the galaxy, meet unexpected danger—"

"Well, you've certainly done that. But look, you haven't been in the service long enough. Give it a chance. It might grow on you."

"I've been in it long enough to know. Of course, I'm sure it's all there in my psychological profile: rebellious, dislikes authority—"

"It doesn't say that at all."

Her expression became curious. "Oh?"

"No. As a matter of fact, it says that you are—" He ticked them off on his fingers, "Intelligent, creative, stubborn, sensitive, telepathic, a practical joker, stubborn, optimistic . . . did I say stubborn?"

"Twice," she giggled.

"Oops, almost forgot—and extremely beautiful."

"That's not in there," she said, lowering her eyes.

"I know. But it's quite true."

"I never noticed."

"I have," he said. And he leaned over and kissed her.

Uhura had made it back from sealing Amanda safely inside her quarters when she returned and found Kirk missing. It was preposterous—there was no way that he could have recuperated that quickly, and yet he had, and she could only hope that he had not been able to stop Spock and the others—but there was no way of knowing. She had cursed herself soundly for not taking the extra precaution of locking him in the small lounge first. After some time of sitting and waiting, she decided to take matters into her own hands and risk looking for Kirk herself. It beat waiting around for him to find her. She had searched for hours on C deck, thinking that the likely place to find him, and had given up in despair and returned to auxiliary. It was then that she saw Kirk waiting for her outside auxiliary. She swore softly under her breath. Luckily, he had not yet caught sight of her, and she pressed her back against the wall of the emergency shaft. Discretion, she decided, *was* the better part of valor, and she angled herself forward just enough to be sure her shot would not miss.

She fired, and Kirk crumpled compliantly on the floor. "Sorry about that, sir," she said sincerely, unable to shake the feeling that she should be court-martialed for what she had just done.

She studied his limp form with indecision. She couldn't leave him outside—he knew where she was, and had obviously been waiting for her. When he came to again, he would alert the others. Besides, she felt a pang of guilt at the thought of leaving him in the hallway, at the mercy of God knows what. She dragged him into auxiliary control and sighed. She most definitely could not leave him in here—she'd have to hit him over the head or stun him each time he revived. The thought struck her as perversely humorous, and she giggled at the insanity of the situation.

It was then that her eyes came upon the small

lounge. She dragged Kirk into the small room, and with a touch of consideration and a lot of grunting, pulled him up onto the couch. She walked outside and pressed the panel that sealed the lounge off, turned, and, resting her back against the door, sank to the floor with a sigh.

The sound of a contrived cough at the entrance to the small cave made McCoy and Anitra break off their embrace immediately. Spock entered with a tray of food.

Anitra brushed a stray lock of hair back. "I'll be back," she murmured and went outside.

Flustered, McCoy straightened his tunic.

Spock set the tray down. "I thought your appetite might have improved, Doctor."

"Hm? Oh . . . yes. Thanks, Spock." McCoy gingerly inspected the contents of the tray. "Anitra was just explaining to me where we are."

"Obviously," Spock said, making McCoy shoot him a guilty glance, but the Vulcan's expression was one of innocence.

McCoy cleared his throat nervously. "How long have we been here?"

"Only four-point-two hours, Doctor. Your recovery has been most rapid."

"I'm sorry I was such a problem. I don't know why the heat got to me so fast. . . ."

"It has nothing to do with you personally. It's a matter of physiology. All humans are affected in the same way by the heat."

"Well, even so, I'm sorry that I held us up."

Spock nodded. "It is an inconvenience."

McCoy reddened. "You don't have to be so damn blunt, Spock."

The Vulcan continued. "I have been thinking about it, Doctor. We can afford no more delays, and quite frankly, you will be of little help to us once we arrive at the academy—you could, in fact, prove to be a hindrance. I have decided that you should stay here, at Gol, where you will be safe. I am sure that the masters would not object."

McCoy struggled to his feet. "Now, wait a minute, Spock. How can you say that a doctor is not worth having around? And I'm perfectly capable of making the trip—"

"Are you, Doctor?" Spock folded his arms resolutely. "It seems to me that you are still weak as a result of exposure. And why should you risk going into the capital? I suggest you consider your own safety. Even if we failed in our mission, you would survive here at Gol."

"Survive—with a bunch of Vulcan mystics. You call that living?"

Spock was silent for a moment. "If I have to order you to stay, Doctor, I will."

"What does the service have to do with it anymore? We're talking about survival here. And I prefer to take my chances with you and Anitra than be left behind."

"As long as I am alive," Spock said slowly, "you will obey my orders."

"Don't pull that crap on me," McCoy replied vehemently. "I'm a doctor, not a soldier, and I'm going with you and Anitra."

"Anitra," Spock echoed, and nodded, one eyebrow lifted.

McCoy blushed deeply. "Yes, and what the hell business is it of yours if I—" He broke off suddenly. "Oh, *now* I get it, Mr. Spock. It has everything to do with Anitra, doesn't it?"

"I don't understand."

"Oh, but you do understand, Spock—only too well. You're jealous, aren't you? I'm moving in on your territory, so you're just going to get rid of the competition by leaving me behind."

"That's absurd," Spock replied simply.

"Is it?" McCoy hissed. "Is it really so absurd, Spock? Maybe deep down somewhere you feel that it's unfair. After all, you've spent a lot of time with her. You probably know her better than I do. And why wouldn't you want her? Her intelligence is a match for yours; she's gifted, she's beautiful . . . she's even mind-linked with you. What more could you want?"

"Doctor, you are rationalizing," Spock said calmly. "The truth of the matter is that you do not wish to remain behind, therefore you cannot admit to yourself that you might be a burden."

"You're a hell of a one to tell me about rationalizing," McCoy answered, glaring. "I won't stay here."

Spock's voice was soft, controlled, the voice of the masters, yet it carried a steely edge that made McCoy swallow any further protests. "You will stay, Doctor—on my order."

He left and did not look back.

Kirk opened his eyes and saw nothing but polished white metal ceiling. He rubbed his face and sat up.

"Where the hell am I?" he asked aloud, but no one replied; the small lounge area was empty. "Anyone here?" he called. No answer. He rose stiffly and walked to the door—and bounced off it when it refused to budge. He struck it with his fist. "Damn it, open!" Nothing. Disconsolate, he walked back to the couch and sat down heavily. It made no sense. What was he doing here? And how had he come to be here in the first place?

He closed his eyes and snatches of memories came back to him. He was with Spock and McCoy in auxiliary control. This must be the small room just off the main control room. But how . . . ? He squinted with the effort to remember. Anitra had been there with them. They had decided to escape on the shuttle-craft, and he was going to trip the circuits to the sensors on the hangar deck. He tried to picture himself on the hangar deck, cutting the circuits, but the image refused to form. Something must have stopped him, something. . . .

He stood up quickly with a shudder. Tomson . . .

"Dear God," he said aloud. But he was somehow himself now. Maybe Spock and Anitra had found the antidote. He walked over to the sealed door again and kicked it. "Spock," he called. "McCoy . . . are you out there?"

Outside, in the main control room, Uhura leaned against the console and pretended not to hear. Kirk—or whatever controlled Kirk—had raved and screamed at first, and then tried to wheedle her into opening the door. It had lasted for hours until the thing had screamed itself hoarse. She had found it extremely unnerving and had to keep reminding herself that it was not the captain talking. The day after, he had remained ominously silent for hours. She'd gone out to raid the commissary for some food—and when she'd come back, Kirk did not even seem to hear the door, but remained perfectly quiet. She was almost glad to hear him talking again, for she had feared Kirk might be dead. But now he took a new approach, one that she found more difficult to deal with.

"Ensign Lanter?" he called. "For God's sake, is anyone out there?" He felt a surge of panic—they had escaped on the shuttlecraft, abandoned the ship and left him sealed inside this small tomb of a room. He forced himself to be calm. Spock was not responsible. Even if he had been possessed, Spock would not have left him like this. Someone else had to have done this—and that someone couldn't be far.

In a flash of inspiration, he decided to cut through the wall, but his phaser was missing from his belt. Then someone must have taken it and thrown him in here. He tried in vain to remember the encounter.

"I know there's someone out there," he called. "Answer me—that's an order."

Uhura had forbidden herself to talk to the thing—but the temptation this time was far too strong; it sounded too much like the captain. "It'll do you no good."

"Uhura," Kirk said, smiling on the other side of the door. "Uhura, let me out of here."

She laughed. "Fat chance."

"For God's sake, Lieutenant, how long have you been keeping me in here."

"A day or so," she said. "Not long enough."

"Uhura, I don't remember what's happened." Kirk pressed himself against the door. "Why are you keeping me here?"

"You tell me," she said, *"Captain."*

162

He fell silent for a moment until an idea occurred to him. "A day or so," he repeated. "Uhura, I'm terribly hungry. If I don't have some food and water soon, I'll die."

She felt a twinge. It was true—and it was a problem that she had tried to avoid thinking about. How could she keep the captain's body alive without facing the thing? She picked up the tray of food that she had gotten for herself, and a cup of water. Balancing it in one hand and a phaser in the other, she went to the door of the lounge.

"All right," she said, "step back from the door. But I'm armed and I swear to God, if you make a wrong move, I won't hesitate to shoot."

"I understand," Kirk said. He stepped to one side and pressed himself against the wall.

Uhura entered, clutching the phaser—but was unable for an instant to see Kirk. He leapt at her, swinging, and the tray clattered to the floor. She fired a wild shot.

It was a clean miss. Kirk had her pinned to the floor in two seconds, but she kneed him square in the crotch, and he fell back, groaning. She groped about for the phaser, but it had slid under the couch where she couldn't see it. His teeth gritted, Kirk crawled over to the couch on his hands and knees and retrieved the phaser.

"Lieutenant," he gasped, sitting on the floor with the weapon pointed at her and fighting the desperate urge to cradle his injured parts, "I promise you, if you ever do that to me again, I'll have you court-martialed."

Uhura looked at him uncertainly; Kirk's eyes were

full of nothing but pain. "Captain, is that really you, sir?"

"I won't do it." McCoy's arms were wrapped tightly about himself in a display of defensiveness. "I won't stay. I can't believe that you're siding with *him* on this."

"Nobody's taking sides." Anitra stood in front of the hot spring, wearing a long, hooded cloak over the softsuit. Soft wisps of steam floated over her reflection in the water; her expression was one of taut control, perhaps out of unconscious emulation of the others. "Don't you understand how dangerous this is?"

"Of course. I've always known. I just can't understand why the two of you would gang up on me—"

"Now you're getting paranoid."

"Maybe I have a right to be."

Anitra sighed and looked into the water. "Don't be ridiculous. I don't want to leave you behind any more than you want to stay. But did it ever occur to you that Spock might be right? It's bad enough that he and I have to risk ourselves by going into the capital—but there's no reason for you to risk yourself."

"To be with you," McCoy said, "is reason enough."

She smiled sadly at him. "But it isn't logical." He started to say something, but she rested her fingertips gently on his lips. "Try thinking that way just for once, Len. If you went with us and something happened to you, I could never forgive myself."

He caught her hand. "And if something happened to you, and I wasn't there to stop it . . ."

"I'll be all right," she said, turning away. "I'll be with Spock."

"I would like to remedy that," he said.

"Please. Promise me you'll stay. It'll only be for a little while."

"All right," McCoy lied. "I'll stay."

"Sorry I had to rush you like that," Kirk said, putting down the phaser.

"I still don't understand, sir," Uhura said. "You were one of them. What happened?"

"You tell me, Lieutenant. What did you do to me?"

"Nothing, sir. Mr. Spock had to stun you. I ran into him in the corridor and he took me back to auxiliary. It seems Ensign Lanter is telepathic and she warned him mentally before we got there that you were in auxiliary. They put you in the lounge, sir, and put Mr. Spock's mother somewhere else. That was about a day and a half ago. I just can't understand why you're yourself again."

Kirk stared at the lounge and shook his head. "Well, I suppose we'll have to brain the entire crew and shove them in there and see if it works."

"With four hundred crew members, that might take a little while, Captain."

"More than that, Lieutenant. What's the status of the ship?"

"We're drifting, sir. Spock sabotaged the engines."

He nodded in approval. "Good. Did Spock and the others make it out of here safely?"

"I have no way of knowing for sure, sir, but if they did, they must be on Vulcan by now."

"What about communications?"

"All out, sir. Ensign Lanter sabotaged them."

"Very good," Kirk murmured. "So . . . a crippled

ship, no communications, and a murderous crew. Looks like we've got our work cut out for us, Uhura. Too bad Spock's not here."

"We'll manage without him, sir."

He grinned at her. "What do you suggest for starters, Lieutenant?"

"For starters? Well, just what you said."

Kirk frowned.

"Brain the whole crew," she said, and giggled.

McCoy cleared his throat, but the Vulcan youth did not stir; he sat in front of the steaming, hot spring, his eyes closed in serene meditation.

"Excuse me," McCoy said.

The Vulcan opened his eyes.

"I need some equipment for crossing the desert," McCoy said.

"It is too dangerous for humans." The Vulcan closed his eyes again.

McCoy persisted. "Look, I've heard all that before. And I'm going anyway. Now, will you help me or not?"

The Vulcan looked up at him. "Your friends asked the High Master for permission for you to stay here. I have heard it said that there is danger outside Gol. Why do you wish to leave?"

"I have been left here against my will."

"Your friends are trying to protect you."

"I don't want to be protected!" McCoy kicked the stone floor in exasperation; a small puff of red dust rose. "I would prefer to risk danger in order to be with my friends. They're risking danger themselves, and I want to help." He eyed the youth warily. "Maybe that's something you Vulcans can't understand."

Soltar looked up at him sharply. "I do understand. As I said before, we aren't keeping you here against your will."

"No . . . but you would let me go out into the desert without any protection."

It seemed for a moment that Soltar would sigh, but he caught himself in time. "If I help you, I will have to inform the High Master."

"You can do that after I'm gone." The Vulcan started to protest, but McCoy cut him off. "There's no time. My friends have already left. If I lose their trail, I'll be lost myself on the desert."

The Vulcan rose with an air of resignation. "I can bring you what you need so that you will not lose your way. Stay here. I will return shortly."

"Thanks," McCoy said, grinning. "Thanks very much."

Sunset. The air was cooling quickly, but McCoy still felt uncomfortably warm in his softsuit and cloak. The boots Soltar had brought made navigating the sand dunes far easier; even so, his ankle ached dully with each step. It was just as well that he had waited before following Spock and Anitra; it had occurred to him that once he got close enough, Anitra might be able to sense his presence. He pulled the old-fashioned compass from a hidden pocket in the cloak, and oriented himself until he faced east-northeast, the direction where ShanaiKahr lay. In the fading light, it gave him comfort to see two sets of footsteps heading in the same direction; the wind, which had howled so devilishly only an hour before, had stilled itself just before sunset so that their trail had not yet been erased.

Somewhere, beyond his line of vision, Spock and Anitra were together. He tried to imagine what they were talking about, and was instantly engulfed by an irrational wave of jealousy. McCoy tried to clear his head; Anitra was probably too far away, but such a precaution couldn't hurt. He concentrated on his pace; they would outdistance him soon if he wasn't careful, and he had no intention of losing them. The wind would stir up soon and erase their footsteps in the sand; McCoy only hoped that Spock's instincts were as good as the compass.

He continued across the sand for some time, breathing heavily from his quickened pace, as the sky darkened and the desert faded slowly to an indistinct gray. The first soft, tentative breeze rustled his cloak and carried the sharp, metallic cry of a le matya. The sound was uncomfortably close, and McCoy stepped up his pace; a moving target, at least, had a better chance.

The le matya screamed again; only this time, it was closer.

"Wait." Anitra stiffened and stopped dead in the sand. Spock waited next to her, listening. "A le matya," he said, "but not close enough to be a threat."

Anitra's face was hidden within the hood of her cloak. "That's not it. It's McCoy."

Spock raised an eyebrow.

"Over there." She pointed in the direction of the le matya's scream.

She broke into a run, and Spock followed; beyond the slow, sloping rise of one dune, and then another, was McCoy, cloaked as they were. Even though he was covered by the loose folds of his garment, Anitra could see that his body was tensed; he had drawn the ahn vahr that Soltar had provided, and his whole attention was focused on the squat, muscular reptile facing him.

Spock cupped his hands around his mouth and gave a short, eerie cry. The le matya turned dully in his direction and sniffed the air with its tongue.

"Doctor," Spock called, "do not move."

But it was too late. McCoy broke into a run the moment the creature was distracted. Spock directed another cry at the le matya, but it was too enraged by the thought of its dinner fleeing. It leaned back on two mighty, rippling haunches and pounced.

"No," Anitra screamed, but it was carried off by the wind.

Spock fired; the brilliant beam from the phaser split the darkness. . . .

But McCoy never saw it.

Chapter Ten

ANITRA FLEW TO McCoy's side and dropped to her knees. "Thank God," she murmured. The doctor sat, conscious but dazed, in the sand.

Spock came over. "Are you all right, Doctor?"

McCoy nodded, half breathless. "I'm okay. It just knocked the wind out of me, that's all."

Spock helped the doctor to his feet.

"I know what you're going to say." McCoy was already on the defensive. "I'm already causing you to lose more time again. But dammit, it was a simple case of bad luck. It could have happened to any of us."

"It would not have happened at all," Spock said stonily, "if you had not disobeyed a direct order. And I am amazed at your capacity for recurring 'bad luck'." His eyes scanned the doctor briefly. "Any scratches?"

"No. I'm glad you came when you did." McCoy looked at Anitra. "Did you know it was me?"

She put a hand on his arm. "Fear travels a long way."

He smiled. "I had enough to get to ShanaiKahr and back. Thanks for noticing." He wobbled slightly.

"What is it?" Anitra said, alarmed.

"It's nothing." McCoy wiped a sudden trickle of cold sweat from his forehead.

Spock caught him before he fell and eased him gently to the ground.

"What's wrong with him?" Anitra cried.

Spock examined McCoy's limp form and pointed to the small scratch on the doctor's wrist where tiny beads of blood were already congealing in the dry air. "The scratch of a le matya is quite poisonous."

"Maybe something in the medikit—" Anitra suggested.

Spock shook his head. "The poison requires a specific antidote. Without it, he will die."

Anitra fought to keep her voice from trembling. "How soon?"

"The cut is superficial . . . an hour, perhaps two."

"An hour—" The words caught in her throat. "Do you think we could get him to a doctor by then?"

"Possibly. But transporting him is dangerous. It could speed the spread of the poison."

"I'll go to the city, then." Anitra was resolute. "I'll bring someone."

"No. I am more familiar with the city. I know where the healer lives."

"Then tell me. I would know if the healer is safe to bring back here." She paused, and in perfect imitation of him, said, "I am the logical choice."

Spock looked down at McCoy's pale face. "Very well," he said. "But you must hurry."

McCoy shivered as the wind swept over him. Spock was sitting so as to block the wind as much as possible, but it still was not enough; he tucked the doctor's cloak more tightly about him and raised the hood so that it sheltered McCoy's face from the wind and sand. Precisely forty-seven minutes ago, Anitra had left, and McCoy had been mercifully unconscious the entire time until a moment before when the delirium had started.

Spock had only twice before seen the effects of a le matya's poison—once, on a pet; the other time, during the ordeal of the *Kahswan,* on a childhood friend. Neither had received help in time to survive. Spock knew that while the poison might affect humans somewhat differently, the doctor would no doubt suffer greatly.

McCoy's face had already turned a distressing shade of gray, and his muscles spasmed periodically, then relaxed, trembling from the effort. His eyelids fluttered, but never opened quite long enough for him to focus on anything. He was speaking now, but the words were so slurred that Spock could barely make them out.

"Anitra," he said. "Don't go. Don't . . ."

"She will be back soon," Spock said. "Don't speak."

"Sorry," McCoy mumbled. "Didn't mean to . . . didn't mean to . . ." He tried to pull himself up, but Spock held him down gently.

"It wasn't your fault you were injured," Spock said, although he doubted the doctor heard or understood.

"My fault," said McCoy. "Didn't mean to love her . . ."

Hardly something to apologize for, Spock thought.

"You mustn't hurt her, understand? Can't let you hurt her—" McCoy broke off, shaken by another spasm of pain. "Isn't fair . . . isn't fair to her. Too many people . . . trying to make her into . . . something she's not. . . ."

Spock listened in the darkness. "I shall keep it in mind, Doctor," he said softly, ". . . if she ever makes it back."

Kirk crouched inside the darkened doorway to Scott's inner sleep chamber, waiting for the moment when the engineer would be off duty. He had picked the lock to the engineer's quarters and carefully re-locked the door behind him. He had been squatting patiently in the dim light, his phaser drawn, for a good fifteen minutes before he heard the door slide open.

His grip on the phaser tightened and he half rose, ready to fire, but stopped before his finger squeezed the trigger.

Tomson entered the outer room. She wore her phaser, an accoutrement not all that unusual for a security chief, but the Klingon dagger—a brutal, three-pronged weapon outlawed in Federation territory—was. She walked slowly about the outer office; she, too, was clearly searching for a place to hide. As she neared Kirk, she paused, and the sudden deliberation with which she moved alerted him to the fact that his presence had been detected. Before she reached either weapon she wore, Kirk had already fired his.

She slumped to the ground.

He stood over her for a moment, thinking. He could

drag her outside Scott's quarters and hide her some-where, with the hopes that Scott would not arrive while Kirk was gone. However, there was also the chance that she might regain consciousness before Scott arrived, and return to reveal Kirk's presence.

He decided not to risk either scenario. He pulled his security chief up over his shoulder. At six feet six inches, she made an awkward bundle; her upper torso hung all the way down his back, and her thin platinum hair, unraveled from its customary knot and hanging forward, swept the floor. Kirk wobbled a bit at first, but managed.

He was quite unable to suppress the smug feeling that he had just gotten even with something.

Anitra ran—flew—over the desert dunes. The wind filled the back and sleeves of the cloak, which she had permitted to fall open, and they flapped and billowed; her hood had long ago fallen back, and she let her hair stream quite unself-consciously. The thought occurred to her that removing the cloak would reduce wind drag, but she could not let herself take the time even for that.

It took her less than an hour to reach the outskirts of the city; in the distance, the multiple pale domes of the academy shone weakly. She stopped for a moment to remember Spock's directions and orient herself.

The sky was virtually empty of traffic, and she was the only pedestrian on the sand streets. She waved to the occasional skimmer that passed overhead, but none stopped, and she wished she had thought to ask Spock the Vulcan gesture for hitchhiking.

Fortunately, the fourth skimmer that passed

stopped in the sky and gently lowered itself beside her. She could see just well enough in the darkness to make out a smiling human face, and she lowered her screens long enough to sense the absence of evil. She returned the smile and climbed into the skimmer.

The hatch lowered as Anitra settled back into her seat; in the glow from the control panel, she was able to make out her host's face. She would have climbed right back out if they hadn't already been a hundred feet off the ground.

"I never thought to see you again," Roy said. If possible, he was drunker than he had been the last time they had met. "I knew it was you the minute you smiled. I've never seen a smile like yours."

The much-touted smile froze on her face. "Roy, isn't it?"

He beamed, pleased that she should remember. "That's right. Aren't you gonna tell me yours?"

"Anitra."

"Anitra. That's a pretty name."

She started to protest, then thought better of it. "Roy, you could really help me. I have a friend in trouble—"

"Not one of them you was with last time," Roy growled. "I don't owe them nothing."

"No," she lied. "Someone else . . . a girlfriend of mine. She got hurt out in the desert. I have to get a healer."

"Hurt, huh? Not bad, I hope."

"Bad," Anitra said. "We've got to hurry." She pointed. "Over in that direction."

"The suburbs, of course." Roy hiccupped. "I suppose I could head this baby in that direction."

"Thank you," she said fervently.

He squeezed his eyes at her sideways. "You know, I hope you're not still mad about what happened."

Anitra bit her lip and decided it would be best to stay on Roy's good side. "Not at all. I notice you're still on Vulcan. I thought you were just on shore leave."

"I decided to extend it," Roy said darkly. "Funny things are going on with the crew—kind of a mutiny, you could say. I thought it'd be safer to stay behind. Of course, it's been getting weird enough around here these days. Vulcans killing Vulcans now, they say. Things like that haven't happened for thousands of years."

He glanced at her in the darkness, but she sat absorbed in her own thoughts.

"I might ask you what you were doing out in the desert at night. It's never been too safe out there."

"That's why we need the help," Anitra said drily. "Look, the important thing is that we get the healer. We can talk later."

"Suit yourself."

They flew along in silence for a moment; Anitra leaned back and watched, hypnotized by the sight of the city passing by beneath them.

"Wait a minute," she said. "We've passed it."

Roy did not seem to hear.

"Turn around. It's back behind us."

Roy continued flying without a word.

"Hey." A note of anger crept into Anitra's voice. "Where do you think you're taking me?"

Roy leered at her. "We'll get you to your healer. I'm just taking the . . . scenic route." He leaned over and put his huge hand on her thigh.

Anitra's hand sought the phaser hidden in the folds of her cloak and closed on it. "Turn this craft around," she said, pulling the phaser out.

Roy's initial astonishment gave way to amused confidence. "Now, look here, honey, you're just a little nervous. I know you wouldn't use that thing on me."

"I'm with Star Fleet Intelligence, you mouth-breathing idiot, and I'll do whatever I have to do to get to a healer. Now turn this goddamn thing around before I blow you away and do it myself."

"Holy . . ." Roy said.

The skimmer came about in a wide arc.

Anitra stood outside the stone wall and pounded on the wooden gate. Vulcans, Spock had told her, rarely, if ever, locked anything, but the healer's doors were sealed shut against intruders. She called out several times, but could not be sure that her cries were not swallowed by the wind.

When she was on the verge of tears and utter desperation, her face leaning against the smooth, polished gate, she heard a voice on the other side of the gate.

"Go away," the healer cried. "Leave me in peace."

"I'm not dangerous," Anitra called. "I don't want to hurt you. My friend was attacked by a le matya on the desert and needs your help."

"Say what you will," came the voice. It was thin, reedy, aged. "I will not open the door. Go."

Anitra's voice rose, impassioned. "You must. My friend will die if you do not come!"

"You are like all the others. Emotional, violent—"

"I'm *not* like all the others. If I sound emotional, it's

because I'm Terran and my friend is dying. Please *hurry.* We don't have time to argue—"

"I will not come." The healer's voice was cold and distant; already he was moving away from the gate.

Anitra sobbed without tears; her face still pressed against the cool gate, she could hear the steps of the healer, walking away.

"Stop!" she called. "If you won't come, then throw me the le matya's antidote over the wall. Do that and I will leave you alone."

There was a silence on the other side of the wall, and she was sure that the healer had gone, already out of earshot. She bowed her head in frustration, but then a voice said on the other side of the fence, "Your friend—is he also Terran?"

"Yes," she said. Her eyes burned with sudden tears.

She heard the soft sound of sand squeaking under his footsteps as he went into the house. A moment later, a small object sailed over the wall onto the sand. The wind began to roll it across the ground. Anitra chased it a short distance and picked it up.

"When you open the vial," the healer called, "inside you will find a hypospray. Use it on your friend and he will live if it is not too late."

"Thank you," Anitra said. "Thank you."

But the healer had already gone back into his house.

There were three long buzzes at the door—the code Kirk and Uhura had agreed upon—and Kirk walked over to the door and stood next to it, his back pressed against the wall. He pushed the panel Anitra had rigged to open the door.

Uhura entered, and Kirk relaxed visibly—but she was alone.

"You're late," he said. "Where's Sulu?"

"I got him without any trouble, Captain, but I need your help in getting him back here. The problem was carrying him down the emergency shaft—" She broke off as Tomson, locked inside the lounge, burst into another tirade of unspeakable threats and obscenities. "Sir, that certainly doesn't sound like Mr. Scott."

"It's not," Kirk answered. "It seems that Lieutenant Tomson had planned her own little surprise for Mr. Scott. Only I was lucky enough to get there first."

Uhura's eyes widened uncertainly.

"Tell me where Sulu is," Kirk said. "I'll go get him."

"I'll go with you, sir," said Uhura. "I'd rather you didn't go alone."

"There's no point in risking both of us, Lieutenant."

"I know, sir, but I'd rather go with you than stay here and listen to *that*." She nodded in Tomson's direction.

Kirk made a wry face. "You have a point there, Lieutenant."

She led him to the emergency shaft that opened just outside C deck, the level of the officers' quarters. "You'll find him at the top of the shaft, Captain."

Kirk entered the shaft first and began to climb the rungs; Uhura followed. Before he could make it all the way up, he saw that Sulu was indeed at the top. Brandishing a fencing foil, he leaned threateningly over Kirk's head.

"How refreshing," Sulu gloated. "Another innocent victim."

Kirk looked down between his feet at Uhura. "Uhura, get out of here! He's come to."

She did not budge.

"Lieutenant, that's an order. Move it! Do you hear me?"

"Oh, I hear you, Captain," she said sweetly, smiling up at him as she trained her phaser on him. "I hear you. But you see, Sulu's promised me a chance to feed."

Spock could see the skimmer lights approaching from some distance away, and from the vessel's heading he was able to surmise that it was heading straight for them. He could only hope that when someone emerged, it would be Anitra.

Fortunately, it was. She was attended by a tall, muscular human male who impressed Spock with his singularly unintelligent expression. He hung back near the skimmer, but Anitra ran to McCoy's side immediately.

"How is he?"

"He's been in a coma for the last five-point-three minutes," Spock said. "I am uncertain whether he can be revived."

Anitra found the hypospray and emptied it into the doctor's arm, but McCoy remained ashen and scarcely breathing.

"It's not working." Alarmed, she looked up at Spock.

"Give it time," Spock said. He ran the mediscanner over McCoy and checked the results, then looked at Anitra.

"His heartbeat is getting stronger."

Anitra sighed and sank back into the sand.

"You lied to me," Roy muttered from a distance. "You said your friend was a woman, but this is the jerk who knocked my tooth out."

Spock raised an eyebrow. "You must be mistaken, sir."

Anitra turned on Roy. "If I'd told you the truth, would you have come?"

"Probably not," Roy admitted.

"Well, I'm grateful you did," said Anitra. "I can't tell you how much."

Abashed, Roy looked at his feet and mumbled something incomprehensible.

McCoy's eyelids fluttered.

"Doctor," Spock said, "can you hear me?"

There was no answer.

"Doctor—"

"I hear you, Spock," McCoy said weakly. "You don't have to shout."

"I was hardly shouting, Doctor. . . ."

McCoy moaned as he sat up and put his head in his hands. "Argh. What a hangover. What happened?"

"The le matya scratched you," Spock said. "You're lucky to have survived."

"Just a scratch did this?"

Spock nodded. "It has venom sacs in its claws. Anitra went to the capital to procure some anti-venin—"

"So that's what's making me so nauseous," McCoy groaned.

"Hmm," said Spock. "I believe that the idiom

181

'the shoe is on the other foot' is rather applicable here."

"My hypos never made you nauseous, Spock," McCoy said, with a small, vehement burst of energy. "That was all in your head."

"I see," Spock replied. "Just as it is in your head now. Regardless of all that, the antidote Anitra obtained saved your life."

Anitra blushed. "Actually, Roy was responsible. I wouldn't have made it back in time if he hadn't—"

"Oh, my God . . ." McCoy paled again as he looked behind Spock and Anitra at Roy. "I knew it. I've died and gone to hell. My grandma always told me this would happen, but I never believed it. . . ."

Roy growled and retreated closer toward his skimmer to show that the feeling was mutual.

"Am I to understand that you know this gentleman, Doctor?"

"Damn straight. The sucker insulted Anitra and gave me a black eye."

"And you cost me a tooth," Roy started to protest loudly.

"A drunken brawl," Spock said with a contemptuous air, "in a tourist bar—"

Anitra stamped her foot. "Shut up, all of you! And you, Doctor—he saved your life. He gave me a ride back here. The least you could do is thank him."

"Thank him," McCoy scoffed weakly. "Not on your life."

Spock leaned forward and said in a low voice, "Doctor, I suggest you treat the young gentleman with more respect. He has a skimmer, which we can use to get to the academy."

"I'd rather die in the desert," McCoy asserted.

"If you would, then you will die alone," Spock said. "I, for one, much prefer to take a skimmer rather than continue our journey on foot."

McCoy considered the alternative for a moment, then turned and addressed himself to Roy, looking for all the worlds as if he had something extremely unsavory in his mouth. "Say there . . . Roy, is it? I didn't mean to be hasty just then. Maybe we can let bygones be bygones. . . ."

Roy let them out in front of the Vulcan Science Academy well before dawn.

McCoy stepped shakily from the skimmer, Anitra and Spock each holding onto an arm. "Well, where is it?"

Spock looked at him quizzically.

"The academy," McCoy repeated. "Where is it?"

"This is it, Doctor."

McCoy looked at the tall, domed buildings stretching out to infinity in every direction. "This isn't an academy, Spock—this is a city."

"It is nearly twice the size of Star Fleet Academy, Doctor, if that is what you're comparing it to." The rows of buildings seemed identical to McCoy, but Spock seemed to know where he was going. He led them, over blessedly unshifting rock, for what seemed to McCoy an interminably long time, until he brought them to the door of one of the buildings. McCoy could not understand how Spock had managed to tell it from any of the others, for the buildings were not numbered; he knew he would never be able to find his way back alone.

In spite of the ungodliness of the hour, the door was unlocked and opened easily. Spock and Anitra drew their phasers; Spock went first, Anitra behind, still clutching McCoy's upper arm with one hand in a gesture of support.

But the halls were empty and quiet. McCoy gave silent thanks for the smooth stone floors, easily navigable in the darkness. Spock led them to a downward staircase; from the first landing they came to, they saw a light coming from that floor, and two Vulcans talking calmly in the hall. The Vulcans turned, saw them, and moved quickly into one of the offices.

"They're all right," said Anitra. "I think they're more worried about us."

They continued walking downward until McCoy's knees began to ache. At last, the stairs went no further. Spock led them to a large room on the right and touched the wall. The room filled with light.

"This is one of the medical labs," Spock said. "I believe it is one of the best equipped."

"No kidding." McCoy whistled. Some of the equipment he could not even recognize. It made sickbay on the *Enterprise* look quaintly old-fashioned.

"I thought you might find it interesting," Spock continued. He pressed another panel on the wall and gray metal walls slid out, covering the old stone ones. The door behind him disappeared.

"What are you doing?" McCoy asked.

"The lab can be sealed or opened by using this panel," Spock answered. A safety feature—in case of a radioactive leak during certain experiments. It cannot be opened, however, from the outside."

"Lucky for us," McCoy muttered.

"You'll find a food synthesizer here," Spock said. "You'll have everything you need."

"You're not going," Anitra said. It was a question.

"Our experiments would be quite useless without a subject."

"You think you're going out there alone to bring someone back?" McCoy asked.

"You're hardly in shape to assist, Doctor," Spock said, with more than a hint of sarcasm. McCoy did not dispute it; his ankle still slowed him down, and he was still weak and queasy from the le matya poison—or was it the antidote?

"You're right," he said unhappily.

"You can't go without me," Anitra said. "I'm the one best suited for finding someone—"

"I already know of someone infected," said Spock.

"But who—" Anitra broke off as she realized the answer. "Your father?"

Spock confirmed her guess by ignoring the question. "I shall attempt to procure a skimmer so that the trip does not take long. I do not intend to walk across the desert this time."

"That's insane!" McCoy exploded. "Your father will kill you, Spock. We know how dangerous he is."

"We can't let you risk something like that," Anitra chimed in. "It makes more sense to use someone in the capital."

Spock gazed at them both calmly. "We already know that my father is affected. Therefore, Anitra need not risk herself. Secondly, we know where he is likely to be, so we do not need to waste time searching

185

for him. Thirdly, his sphere of influence is enormous; he can cause tremendous harm to the planet. That alone is an important reason to stop him."

"You're going all the way out to your parents' house to bring him back?" McCoy asked. "Spock, I think that's the most illogical thing you've ever suggested."

A minute change in Spock's expression indicated that the insult had registered. "It is not far by skimmer, Doctor. And the testing may, at times, be quite dangerous for the subject. Are you willing to inflict that on an unconsenting stranger?"

"It's a chance for them—"

"There's a risk in any type of testing. I know that my father would be willing to take the risk."

McCoy shook his head. "It still doesn't make sense to me."

"All right," Anitra said. "You can go—as long as I go with you."

"No," said Spock. "We need you to set up the lab."

"McCoy can handle it."

Spock sighed. "You know best what type of experiments to set up for. Admitted, my father is dangerous. But we cannot risk losing you, Anitra. If the two of us are killed, Vulcan's fate is in the hands of McCoy." The two of them turned and looked at the doctor.

Anitra sighed. "I suppose you're right," she said.

"Well, thanks a *lot* for the vote of confidence," McCoy said.

Spock ignored him. "Before you let me in again," he said to Anitra, "use the mind link. Understand?"

She nodded as he pushed the panel. The door opened briefly, then closed behind him.

"We're crazy to let him go," McCoy said to her.

"The whole thing is crazy," said Anitra. "But I know why he has to go."

McCoy looked at her.

"It's a family thing," she said. "He is responsible to stop Sarek before he kills again."

Chapter Eleven

KIRK TOOK A deep breath and let go of the rungs. His momentum knocked Uhura and she fell, squawking, beneath him. She struck the landing first, but did not entirely break his fall. He fell sideways across her, his back and side striking the floor. For a moment he lay stunned, the wind knocked out of him, but the memory of Sulu galvanized him into action. He stood up, sucked in a deep breath and winced—a rib was broken.

Still unconscious, Uhura lay half in the shaft landing, half in the corridor, and Kirk bent over her, but the sound of Sulu climbing down the shaft stopped him. He found Uhura's phaser on the other side of the corridor and picked it up—no point in leaving it for Sulu.

Sulu stepped over Uhura with a singular lack of concern for his injured comrade and faced Kirk in the corridor. He carried the long rapier in his teeth. Kirk noticed he also wore a phaser, and he decided to fire his own before Sulu could get to it. Sulu fell.

Kirk leaned against the wall, gasping, each breath exquisite misery. He looked at the corridor; he was on C deck, officers' quarters, and damn lucky that no one had been passing by to see what had happened. C deck usually bustled with activity, but now it was silent, as though those who frequented its halls had shut themselves away. Kirk deemed it a good thing, as his broken rib ruled out any possibility of carrying two bodies down the emergency shaft to auxiliary.

He tried to bend down toward Uhura, gave it up, and knelt, his back ramrod straight, beside her. Her pupils were not dilated, and she would probably come to shortly, although he could not be sure without a mediscanner. She seemed to have no serious injuries, save for a wrist that was already swelling to alarming proportions. He rose with difficulty.

Slowly, grimacing, he grabbed Sulu's ankles and began dragging him in the direction of his quarters.

The security system was still on, but the gate yielded to Spock's code. He felt a faint surprise; he had fully expected Sarek to change it, but apparently his father did not fear his return. It was quite possible, Spock reflected glumly, that he welcomed it.

He walked slowly through the gate and did not flinch as it closed behind him. Before him, the door to the house opened invitingly. The sensors recognized him, welcomed him, anticipated his every move, and if Sarek was taking the trouble to monitor them, then he also knew his son was here.

And he was waiting.

Spock came to a halt at the sight of the central room. Even in the weak light, he could see things that were disturbing. The portrait of mother and son hung rightside up in its proper place, but it had been slashed on the diagonal with a sharp weapon. The furniture had not been disturbed, but the large white sofa that his mother had brought with her from Terra was stained with huge splotches of dark green. Spock's eyes followed the blood across the soft carpet and back toward the guest rooms. In the gray light, it was impossible for him to tell how old the stains were; he walked over to the sofa and touched it with his hand. It was cool and dry. Unconsciously, he wiped his hand on his pants as he stood quiet, listening.

All within was silence.

With careful steps he moved to the garden window, to see if Sarek was in his customary place of meditation, but the stone bench was empty.

It occurred to him then that his father might be dead.

He forced himself to follow the bloody trail back to the guest rooms. It led to the room where Anitra had slept. Standing before the door, he became uncomfortably aware of the smell, and had to argue with himself for a full minute before he was able to go in.

When the body pitched forward, he jumped backward a good three feet.

The corpse that hit the carpeted floor with a soft thud was that of a middle-aged Vulcan male whom Spock recognized as one of Sarek's acquaintances from the academy. Rigor mortis had already set in, and in the heat there was already the subtle scent of incipient decay. Spock did not bother to examine him to determine the cause of death; he already knew more than he cared to about how the man had died. He backed away from the corpse without touching it, calm, but beneath the overlay of logic there was a growing thread of fear and revulsion, a low hum, like the soft beating of insects' wings.

It increased as he made his way back to the central area. The door to his parents' bedroom was open, and he went inside. Unlike the other rooms, all was in order here—the room was neat—too neat, as though it had not been inhabited for several days. On the low dresser across from the untouched bed was a hologram of Spock's parents: Sarek stern in full ambassadorial dress, Amanda smiling beside him. Spock stood gazing at the picture, captivated for a moment by the way they had been.

There was a sound from outside the room, soft, almost inaudible, but enough to make Spock spin about toward the door with the phaser.

No one was there. The sound had emanated from another room, most likely Sarek's study.

The door to the study was closed. Spock walked toward it silently until he stood as close as he possibly could without opening it. He aimed the phaser at chest level and charged.

The sight of his father made him freeze. Sarek sat at his terminal, slumped down in the chair, and for a moment, Spock thought he was another corpse until he stirred, struggling to speak. His skin was drained of color, and his eyes were sunken above deep circles. He looked at his son, and it seemed to Spock that the eyes belonged once again to his father. They were trying to tell him something, but Spock could not interpret the message—for although they were Sarek's eyes, they were at the same time different, clouded with alien emotions Spock had never seen in his father before: fear and pleading.

Sarek attempted to lift his head, but the effort required was too great and he let it fall back again. His lips worked silently for a moment before he was able to form words.

"Help me," he said.

"Father?" Spock said. He moved closer; Sarek did not stir in his chair.

"Help me," Sarek croaked.

"What do you want me to do?" Spock asked.

"Help me up," Sarek said. He extended a trembling hand.

Spock reached for the hand—then stopped. He stood helplessly for a moment, teetering on the edge of indecision.

Sarek spoke again, his voice gentle, persuasive, the voice of a diplomat. "Don't fear me, Spock. You do not need to fight me any longer."

For the first time in his life, Spock acted on a sheer hunch. He raised the phaser at Sarek.

Sarek's eyes bored into his. "Put the phaser down, Spock. You will not harm me. You are my son."

"You are not my father," Spock said.

Sarek closed his eyes and sighed heavily. The sun was beginning to clear the shadows from the room, and Spock could see the lines etched in his father's face. Sarek spoke again, his voice deep with weariness. "If I am not your father, then who am I?"

"I do not know. But my father does not kill." Spock steeled himself to fire the phaser; any further conversation with the demon would be pointless, not to mention hazardous.

But before he did, Sarek groaned, clutching at his heart, and crumpled further into the chair. Spock could not resist the instinct to lean closer to his father, and at that instant, Sarek knocked the phaser from his hand with a mighty blow. Spock watched as it sailed across the room. The chair fell backward as Sarek, miraculously recovered, rose to his feet.

A thought flashed across Spock's mind. In a contest of sheer strength, he was no match for his father.

Spock scrambled for the phaser and almost succeeded, but Sarek kicked him in the jaw with such force that it sent him flying backward. He shook his head to clear it and once again made a move for the phaser. Sarek lunged at him, forcing him to roll quickly out of the way.

Spock had hoped that it would not come to this: he had already promised himself that he would not harm Sarek—or more precisely, Sarek's body.

"Father," he said and reached out mentally, desperately, to see if anything of his father remained.

Sarek stopped momentarily and blinked.

But all Spock found was darkness and a black terror that made him tear away in fear that it would veil his own mind.

Sarek roared and charged; Spock, still recovering from his attempt to contact his father, reacted a split second too slowly. Sarek caught him and threw him against the stone wall. There was a sharp crack as Spock's head impacted with the wall. He slid, unconscious, to the ground.

"So what do you think our chances are?" McCoy asked.

Anitra was busy checking the calibration on the decompression chamber and did not look up. "Of what?"

"Of making it out of here."

She looked up at him. "What, out of the medical lab?"

"You're getting to be more like Spock every day," McCoy noted irritably. "Getting too literal. You know what I mean. Surviving. Finding a way to get rid of those things."

Anitra studied the gauge dispassionately. "What kind of question is that, Doctor? Would you like me to do what Spock does and calculate the odds for you?"

"God, no. I suppose I was just trying to find a little reassurance."

She sighed and gave up her attempt at working. "Frankly, Doctor, I don't see any point in talking about our chances. I think such talk is far too depressing."

"I see," McCoy said, disheartened.

"Don't get me wrong. There are plenty of Vulcan scientists out there, probably many of them doing what we are now. Eventually, someone will come up with a solution."

"Eventually," said McCoy, "may be too late."

"Exactly my point," she said, folding her arms in front of her. "That's why I was trying to get this damn thing calibrated. Now are you going to help me or not?"

McCoy had two choices: to get angry or to laugh and help her. He laughed.

"That's better." She brightened. "You've had a pretty rough time on Vulcan so far, haven't you?"

"It's not a nice place to visit. God forbid I should live here."

She laughed; it had a startlingly lovely effect on her

features, and he walked over to smooth her hair with his hand. She did not protest.

"What can I do to help?" he asked, smiling.

"You're the boss in the medical lab," she admitted. "I'm more at home with physics. But you might want to check on the radiation shields in the isolation chamber."

"Will do." McCoy went over to the control console. As he began working, his brow furrowed. He began to say something, then stopped himself.

"All right," Anitra said. "What is it?"

"Well . . . I hate to keep bringing up morbid subjects, but what happens if Spock doesn't make it back?"

"He'll make it back," Anitra said firmly.

"Telepathy is a fact," McCoy said, "but I've never believed in precognition. You don't know that, Anitra."

"I know Spock," she said simply. "I know he'll find a way to make it back."

"And if he doesn't?"

Her expression saddened and she looked away. "Then we go out and find ourselves a subject, Doctor. What else would you expect us to do?"

He got up and walked up behind her chair. "Look, I'm sorry if I'm upsetting you. . . ." He put his hands on her shoulders.

She leaned back against him. "I'm not upset."

"You're right about Spock. I'm sure he'll make it." He leaned forward and kissed her. She returned the kiss, but after a moment, pulled out of the embrace.

"Hey," he said, "is there something wrong? I thought before that . . ."

She sat up straight and turned to face him. "No offense, Len, but we *do* have important work to do. We can't afford to take time out for—"

"Little wonder you have an ulcer," McCoy teased gently, trying not to sound injured. He raised his hands in a gesture of surrender. "No problem. I'll just go back to my console and look pitiful."

"You do that," she said, all business.

They worked in uncomfortable silence for a time. Suddenly, Anitra stood up so quickly that her chair scuttled backward and nearly toppled over.

McCoy looked up in alarm. "What's wrong?"

Fear clutched at her throat so tightly that she was barely able to squeeze the words out. "It's Spock."

"What's wrong? Is he hurt?"

"He . . ." she gasped, unable to get enough air to speak, ". . . he simply isn't *there* anymore."

"What the devil are you talking about?"

"We—we mind linked some time ago. That way each is aware of the other at all times; each can know if the other becomes affected or is in danger."

McCoy took her hand and tried to calm her. "I know, Spock told us. . . ."

She looked up at him and blinked back tears. "Don't you understand? He's gone."

"Take it easy," said McCoy. "All right, he might be dead. But could something else break the link? Could something else have happened?"

Anitra took a deep breath and concentrated. In a voice that was much calmer, she said, "He can't dissolve the link without my presence, so there's no way he can consciously break it. He might be unconscious."

"Asleep, maybe?"

"No, not asleep. I would know his dreams."

McCoy raised his eyebrows but said nothing.

"He's either dead or unconscious. If it's the latter, it means he's hurt somewhere." She pulled her hand away from McCoy and went over to the panel and pressed it. The metal walls began to recede. "And I'm not going to sit here and wonder which one it is."

"Now, just wait a minute," McCoy called, frowning.

Anitra shot him a look that dared him to stop her.

"I'm coming with you," he said meekly.

There had come a merciful hour of silence when Tomson had stopped ranting, and Kirk had been grateful for the silence. He drifted off to sleep until he was awakened by a small, persistent knocking.

"Is anyone out there?" Tomson called.

Kirk rose stiffly to his feet and swore as the broken rib reminded him of its presence. He went to the console and checked the chronometer; it had been roughly twenty-eight hours since the security chief had been incarcerated. He went over to the lounge door and opened it, but not without first drawing his phaser as a precautionary measure.

Tomson sat on the floor by the door, looking particularly pathetic and disheveled. Her uniform had bunched up around her waist, and the retentive bun she wore her hair in had disintegrated into a mass of pins and tangles.

"Sir?" she said curiously, and out of a sense of military protocol began straightening her hair and uniform. The response was so typical of Tomson that

Kirk hung the phaser back on his belt and helped her to her feet.

"If you don't mind my asking, Captain, how the hell did I get in there?"

"It's a long story," Kirk said, grinning with the relief that he was no longer the only sane human on board. "Too long."

"I was in Stryker's quarters. . . ." Her expression slowly became one of realization. "Stryker . . . he hypnotized me or something, sir. He's the one who's responsible for al-Baslama's death. I'm sure of it."

"I don't doubt it," Kirk said soberly. "Only Stryker himself isn't responsible."

"Sir?"

"Some sort of infection, Lieutenant. Or an entity using Stryker. But not Stryker. You and I have both suffered from its effects ourselves."

Tomson's pale eyes grew larger. "You mean I . . ."

"And most of the crew by now, I think. Whoever, whatever they are, they've taken over the bridge. We're sealed off here in auxiliary control."

"Are we still orbiting Vulcan?"

Kirk shook his head. "We're not far from there, but Spock sabotaged the ship so she'd drift. Communications are out, too. We didn't want to risk spreading this thing."

"So you're saying we're trapped on the ship with most of the crew under the influence of . . ."

"Something. I don't know what, but something that causes them to be violent."

Tomson shivered. "Any chance we could get off the ship?"

Kirk stopped; since Spock and the others had gone,

the idea had simply not occurred to him. It smacked too much of desertion. "No. Both shuttlecrafts are gone. And we're not close enough to anything to transport down."

"What sort of plan do you have, sir?"

Kirk paused. "I need my bridge crew back first. Once I have them, I can do anything with the ship."

Tomson confronted him with those freezing-blue eyes of hers. "Sir, you still haven't answered my question about how I got here."

"I brought you here, Lieutenant. I was . . . repaying a favor, you might say."

Tomson flushed. "When I was . . . affected, do you know if I . . . hurt anyone?"

Kirk half smiled. "Well, I happen to know that you gave me a run for my money."

"Sir?"

"It's not important, Tomson. What's important is that we get the bridge crew back."

"Any suggestions on how to do that, Captain?"

"I've already started on it. And you can help."

He took her via the emergency shafts to C deck (and his broken rib made him swear under his breath the entire climb up). There was the sound of a loud fracas in the hallway, and they clung to the ladder silently for a while until it broke up. When the way was clear, they headed for Sulu's quarters. Kirk stopped at the door.

"If my calculations are right, to quote Mr. Spock, they've been in there approximately twenty-eight hours. That was the amount of time it took you to come to your senses. They ought to be all right."

"You mean, all you had to do was shove me in the lounge for twenty-eight hours and I was fine?"

"It seems to be that simple."

"Too simple," Tomson said.

"We'll see." Kirk called softly at the door, "Uhura? Sulu? Can you hear me?" There was no reply. Kirk tried again, but feared raising his voice too loud. "They're in there," he said over his shoulder to Tomson. "There's no way they could have gotten around that lock." He pressed his ear to the door; he could just barely make out the sounds of Uhura moaning softly. He remembered the fall she had taken and opened the door immediately. His phaser was still on his belt, but Tomson, the quintessence of security, held hers at waist level (which guaranteed that it would hit most others directly on the chest).

Uhura lay on the bed in the inner room, exactly where Kirk had placed her the day before. When she saw Kirk, she struggled to hold up her head.

"Captain," she said sweetly.

"Uhura, are you all right?" Kirk moved toward her. "You took quite a fall—"

As he entered the inner room, Sulu leapt from behind the wall and jumped him.

Tomson could not shoot until the two separated. When she did, and Sulu lay twitching on the floor, Uhura came charging. She never had a chance. Tomson fired almost leisurely; the communications officer dropped one step away from Kirk.

"Thanks," Kirk said. He was still breathing heavily from the shock to his injured side. "It's nice to have a bodyguard for a change."

"That's what we're here for," Tomson said, putting her phaser back on her belt. "Did you miscalculate the time, Captain? Did we come too early?"

Kirk folded his arms protectively about his rib cage. "No. I gave plenty of time, even allowed extra. Something's not working here."

"Maybe you should have used the lounge," Tomson suggested. "Maybe there's something special about it."

"It's worth a try," Kirk said.

Tomson hoisted Sulu over her shoulder in a graceful move that wasted little effort. She paused, waiting for Kirk to do the same with Uhura.

Kirk contemplated the picture of Tomson with a body slung over each shoulder . . . and himself, empty-handed, and decided not to explain the rib to her. He bent down, grimaced and pulled Uhura awkwardly over his shoulder.

He wondered how the hell he was going to make it down the emergency shaft.

Spock awoke to the sensation of warmth on his face; the sun was streaming in the window of his room, filling it with intense light. For a moment, he was in the past, a boy in ShiKahr, wondering why his parents had permitted him to sleep so late this particular morning. He began to call for Ee-Chaya, his father's old pet sehlat, but stopped at the realization that Ee-Chaya had died some thirty years before.

He looked around the room and was struck by a wave of nausea. The light pained his eyes and he closed them. Obviously, he had injured his head. But what was he doing at his parents' house?

He tried to rise and crawl onto his bed, but could not. He was somehow restrained into a sitting position, his hands behind him, his knees bent. It was then that he remembered the body that had fallen in the doorway and the struggle with his father.

Sarek would no doubt be returning for him soon.

It occurred to him that he should contact Anitra, but after some consideration he decided there was no logic in risking her as well. It would be better to keep his thoughts from her as best he could. She and McCoy were safe in the lab where they should be. When he was dead, she would know it and then find another subject. He trusted her to find a solution.

He prepared himself for death and promptly fell asleep.

Chapter Twelve

"HE'S ALIVE," ANITRA crowed triumphantly. "I just got a sensation then. . . ." She was sitting behind the control panel of the skimmer they had found parked in the street not far from the academy. In typical Vulcan fashion, it had been left unlocked—in fact, it was made entirely without locks—and she was trying to figure out how to start it.

"Where is he?" McCoy turned toward her in his seat and leaned forward. "Is he with Sarek?"

"I don't think so." She frowned. "I don't think he knows where he is. He's not making it easy for me."

"What do you mean?"

"He's trying to shield his thoughts from me, but he's not doing a very good job of it. There . . . he's asleep right now."

"Asleep? That doesn't make sense," McCoy said. "Well, at least he's alive. That's what's important."

Anitra smiled in agreement and turned her attention once again to the control panel of the skimmer. "I watched Roy drive one," she said. "They're really quite simple." She looked over at McCoy. "If you read Vulcan, that is."

McCoy feigned irritation. "Wait a minute, you're supposed to be the genius around here. You'd better hurry up and figure this thing out."

Anitra, her face still radiant, let a few fingers fly over the controls, and the skimmer rose spasmodically. "See? Nothing to it."

"Fine. Now, if you could just lower it enough to pick up my stomach—"

"Sorry about that. The ride should smooth out." Anitra looked through the wide windshield at the skyline and frowned. "Now, all I have to do is figure out which direction ShiKahr is. . . . That way." The skimmer accelerated spasmodically.

McCoy groaned. "Can't you put this thing on automatic?"

She looked at him, shocked. "Automatic? Doctor, that would be cheating."

"This is it," Anitra said. The windshield on the skimmer lifted up and she hopped out. McCoy crawled out gingerly, his legs rubbery after what Anitra had called "an exhilarating ride."

Anitra stood before the gate of Sarek's house and held her hand before the metal plate. Nothing happened.

"Security must be on," she muttered. "I wouldn't be surprised if he's changed the code."

"We can't get in?" McCoy asked hopefully.

Anitra didn't answer; she thought for a moment, then touched the plate in what seemed to McCoy like a perfectly random sequence. The gate slid open.

"How'd you do that?" McCoy demanded.

"Good memory."

She started inside, but he put a hand on her shoulder and held her back. "Look, do we have any sort of plan? That is, do we know what we're getting into?"

McCoy had always had an innate half-buried fear of Vulcans. Perhaps it had something to do with their severe appearance, or the hint of a fierce warrior past, coupled with bone-crushing strength. Whatever the reason for it, McCoy knew he was afraid to face Sarek—even more terrified than the moment he had realized Jim was lost.

Anitra turned to face him, her hair turned to fire by the Vulcan sun. She frowned in the brightening light, looking every bit as fiercely unapproachable as Sarek himself could ever hope to be.

"Afraid?" Her tone was neutral; McCoy was unsure whether the question was a reproach or a show of sympathy. He nodded reluctantly. "So am I," she said matter-of-factly. "But you're forgetting something important: Spock is in there."

"Uh-huh," McCoy said unenthusiastically.

"If you stay with me, you'll be all right. I'm lowering all my shields. I'll know exactly where everyone in this house is."

"Sounds fair enough to me," McCoy said, and without further argument, he let her lead the way through the gate.

The rooms were now all brightly illuminated, but to McCoy, the house seemed as eerie as if it had been cloaked in shadows. They walked through the entry hall into the central room, Anitra slightly in front, and stopped at the sight of the blood spattered on the couch.

"Spock?" McCoy whispered.

Anitra's expression was grim; she said nothing for a moment, but closed her eyes. When she opened them, she pointed in the direction of the guest rooms and said, "Spock is that way. Sarek is in the study."

McCoy stared, wide-eyed, in the direction of Sarek's study and swallowed. He felt no small sense of relief when Anitra headed in the opposite direction for Spock. His relief was short-lived. They entered the hallway toward the bedrooms and had taken only a few steps when Anitra froze. She turned back toward McCoy and grabbed his arm tightly, but she did not make a sound.

One of the rooms was open, and in its doorway lay a corpse—male, Vulcan, covered with dried blood. "It's all right," Anitra said very, very softly. She was shaken and pale, but her features were composed. "It's not him." She held onto McCoy's arm and led him past the dead Vulcan.

When they had made it as far as Spock's room, she stopped in front of the door. "In here, I think. It's hard to tell—I get a very weak signal, like he's not really conscious."

They entered. Spock sat inside, propped up in a corner, facing the sunlight streaming in through a window. His head hung forward onto his chest, and his hands were restrained behind him. McCoy made it to him first and groped for his scanner. He read the results and looked over his shoulder at Anitra, who was leaning forward and no longer able to suppress an expression of concern—and perhaps something more.

McCoy paused for a moment when he saw the look in her eyes and cleared his throat. "We've got to get him to—" he almost said "the ship," but corrected himself in time, "—the medical lab. He's got a hairline skull fracture. He needs more help than I can give him here."

"Will he die?" Anitra seemed to be steeling herself for the worst.

"Not if we can get him back to the academy in time."

"How much time do we have?"

"Not long," McCoy admitted.

Anitra nodded and stood up; she checked the setting on her phaser. "I'm sorry we only have one weapon," she said, her expression becoming carefully neutral once again. "But I think you'll be all right here with Spock."

McCoy stood up. "Where the devil do you think you're going?"

"To get Sarek." Her eyes dared him to stop her. "That's what we came here for, isn't it?"

"Yes, but we sure as hell didn't agree that you would face him alone—"

"You're forgetting something, Doctor. I've got the element of surprise. I know where he is, and I can figure out most of what he's thinking. But he won't know I'm coming. I'll walk right in the door and stun him before he knows what's happened."

"I'm not going to let you go alone," McCoy repeated adamantly.

"We've got one weapon. What good will it do two people? Besides, are you going to leave Spock here like this?"

"I don't like it." He realized he was beaten and cast about for a better argument, but there was none. She was right.

She smiled in an unconvincing attempt to encourage him. "I'll be back in a minute."

He did not smile back. He simply watched as she walked out the door and it slid shut behind her. "Good luck," he said.

Spock's head began to sway from side to side; he moaned with the effort required to lift it and let it fall back against the wall. His eyelids fluttered.

"Spock?" McCoy asked gently.

Spock mumbled something so softly that at first McCoy did not understand. "Anitra," he said.

"She's here, Spock," said McCoy. "You're going to be all right."

Spock's eyes opened wide for a moment and looked lucidly at McCoy. "Sarek," he said suddenly. "She must not go——" He closed his eyes as though speaking caused his headache to intensify.

"She'll be all right," McCoy comforted, but Spock had already fallen asleep again. If they did not get him to the lab soon, he would slip into a coma.

McCoy heard the sound of a phaser somewhere, far away, and fancied he also heard a body fall on the soft carpet. He sighed, taking comfort in the sound. He was already trying to figure out how to arrrange the two unconscious Vulcans in the skimmer when he noticed something. Spock's phaser was missing from his belt. McCoy knew, without a doubt, that he had taken one with him when he first left to retrieve his father; and for what McCoy told himself was no good reason, his hands began to shake. He folded them tightly under his arms and scolded himself for being so overimaginative.

Still, he could not seem to stop shaking. Time

seemed to slow after the sound of the phaser fire; to pass it, McCoy tried to picture what Anitra was doing. First, she stood over Sarek's body for a moment to be sure he was unconscious; perhaps she even examined him. Then she grabbed him by his heels and began to drag him toward the central room. She would take him almost to the front door before she would stop to go back and tell McCoy to come. He imagined all this, counting the seconds for each action, allowing more than ample time. And yet, she was taking too long—far too long. His nerves, of course, had altered his perception of time—a perfectly natural phenomenon.

But it really *was* taking her too long. He looked over at Spock: the Vulcan was resting quietly. There was nothing McCoy could do to help him right now, even if anything happened. The doctor scraped up the last ounce of his courage and headed for the door. He would go look for her. If Sarek had her, there would be nothing he could do—but at least he would know. At least he wouldn't sit waiting in the room for something to happen.

But before he reached the door, there were soft footsteps outside. "Anitra?" he asked as the door slid open.

He took a step backward before his legs buckled under him. Sarek looked as hellish as McCoy had pictured him in his worst nightmares—his eyes burned black in a sunken, yellowed face, and he held McCoy with a gaze that stopped the doctor's heart. McCoy waited for the change, waited to become as Sarek was, but nothing happened to him. In a pitiful gesture, hoping to appeal to whatever was left of Spock's father, he nodded at Spock and said in a voice so weak he could scarcely hear it himself, "He'll die soon unless we get him some help."

"A pity," the Vulcan said in a voice that was Sarek's and yet not Sarek's.

He stepped forward through the doorway so that McCoy could see what was behind him. McCoy was too stunned, too shocked to react. He merely stared.

Anitra stepped forward into the doorway. She looked just the same, but when she smiled it was subtly changed. "Hello, Doctor," she said.

"Well," said McCoy, "get it over with."

Anitra looked confused for a moment. "Get it over . . . ah, take you, you mean." The insincere smile returned. "But we don't need you, Doctor—not that way. We need you for other things."

She looked so much like herself, McCoy felt an odd tug of love—and hatred—for her. He made his best attempt at bravado. "What kind of things?" he demanded.

"Are you really sure you want us to go into detail? I suppose it doesn't really matter." She looked at Sarek.

"We needed the female," Sarek said, "for ourselves. She makes us very powerful. We need you . . . to feed."

"Oh," McCoy said weakly. He was reminded all at once of some very bad old science-fiction books he had read as a kid. "That's all right. Maybe I really don't need that much detail. . . ."

Anitra laughed, a hard, metallic sound. "Such a literal mind you have, Doctor. Just think of what happened on the *Enterprise*. I'm sure you'll figure it out."

"So you've come to kill us," McCoy said. "Why don't you take me and leave Spock alone? He can't harm you."

"Oh, we'll leave you both alone . . . for the moment," she answered. "Spock is certainly no use to us in his present condition. We need him to get better and we need you to be in charge of that. We can bring you whatever you need."

McCoy felt a sudden disgust. "What are you going to do? Make him better so that you can kill him? I won't do it."

She leaned forward, hissing. McCoy could not refrain from drawing back. "You'll do what I tell you to."

Spock stirred slightly and McCoy looked down at him. His eyes were open, clear and lucid, and they looked directly at Anitra. He did not speak, but clearly knew exactly what had happened. He closed his eyes again with utter resignation.

McCoy's tone changed. "Why don't we make a deal?"

Anitra looked at him, amused.

"I'll take care of Spock if you promise to let him go. You can keep me."

The grating laughter came again. "You forget, Doctor, I know your thoughts. You have no intention of letting Spock die."

"Have you forgotten your Hippocratic oath, Doctor? And you are in no position to bargain. Although we prefer Spock alive for the moment, it makes only a small difference to us."

McCoy stared up at Sarek, aghast at the words coming from his lips.

He continued, "Ultimately, the outcome for you and Spock will be the same."

"Think about it while we're gone," Anitra said. "I'll be back soon."

And they were gone.

McCoy knelt by Spock's side and put a hand on his friend's arm. "I'm sorry," he said inaudibly and bowed his head. Anitra knew what was in his heart, but he could not weaken and follow it this time.

He would have to let Spock die.

Anitra had managed to bring McCoy what he had asked for, and other than a few veiled hints at their ultimate fate, seemed content to leave him and Spock in peace. It was as though she wished to prolong the agony of anticipation for as long as she could.

And it had been nothing less than agony for McCoy. He sat for hours staring at the hypospray that would sustain Spock long enough to get him to surgery—but as yet had not yielded to the temptation to use it. And that temptation was becoming very great. He pulled out the scanner for the hundredth time in the past hour and ran it over the Vulcan. Spock's heartbeat had slowed . . . the Vulcan had finally slipped into a coma. There was little time left; if McCoy wanted to change his mind, he would have to do it now.

The doctor rose, his arms folded tightly, his hands gripping his sides, and paced around the room. The light was dimming rapidly; on the other side of the house, windows were streaming with the rays of the setting sun. On the other side of the house, Anitra knew everything McCoy was feeling, and sat, waiting. He closed his eyes and tried to blank his mind, but he could not erase the image of the dying Vulcan. He owed it to Spock to save his life . . . but his mind filled with the gruesome image of al-Baslama on the autopsy table. No, he argued with Anitra silently, he could not let the same thing happen to Spock. He looked over at the Vulcan. Spock was still restrained in the corner, his head sagging once again onto his chest, and McCoy realized just as certainly that he would not permit the Vulcan to die now, either.

"I won't let it happen," he said. "Dammit, Spock, I refuse to let it happen." He went to the Vulcan's side and administered the hypospray. Somewhere, he knew, Anitra would be smiling at her victory.

And then something very strange happened. Spock's heartbeat sped up, almost to its normal rhythm, and then . . . it stopped. McCoy closed his eyes. He no longer had a choice to make. Spock was dead. He let the anger and grief fill his mind; he wanted Anitra to feel the depth of it.

When she came into the room, he was ready for her—pressed against the wall next to the doorway. But his mind was over by Spock, grieving. He was by no means good at hand-to-hand combat—such skills were not required of medical personnel in the service—but desperation made him very accurate. Mindlessly, he struck out so that the phaser dropped from her wrist, and he made sure that he was the first to reach it. Sarek was on her heels, and McCoy decided to save explanations until after everyone was unconscious on the floor.

"I'm sorry, my dear," he said. "You shouldn't believe everything people think."

* * *

"Dammit!" Kirk struck the top of the console with his fist, making Tomson jump. "What are we doing just sitting here? Waiting for Spock to come back and rescue us?"

"Do you think he'll make it, sir?" Tomson asked miserably. Until a moment ago, the two of them had sat in unconscious imitation of each other, slumped over, their cheeks resting on their fists in a gesture of despair.

It hadn't worked with Sulu and Uhura. Thirty hours after their incarceration, they were still fighting each other to the point that Kirk risked opening the door to stun them both, just to keep them from tearing each other apart. For the moment, the two were quiet, but the effects of the phaser blast would no doubt wear off soon. It had not been easy for Kirk to accept the fact that he would not have his bridge crew back. He was alone, except for Tomson—and at the moment, he could not see the advantage of her presence.

"He'll make it," Kirk said with so much conviction that he almost convinced himself. "But do you want to sit here in auxiliary control hoping Scotty doesn't find a way in here before Spock gets back? God knows how long that might be."

"Not particularly, sir." Tomson seemed unenthusiastic at the prospect. "Did you have a suggestion?"

"I know where Spock put the device that's causing the engines to stall," said Kirk. "I can disengage it so we can have some power."

"But what's the point, sir? I thought Spock put it there so we can't contaminate anyone else. Isn't it a little risky, running around the galaxy with a shipful of—"

"With the transporters and communications out, what kind of threat are we? Besides, there are ways to seal off certain decks."

She glumly leaned her chin on her fist again. "And how do we convince a shipload of berserk crewmen to go to certain decks? Anyway, we've seen how they treat each other in close quarters. They'd kill each other."

"They're killing each other now," Kirk reminded her grimly. "Dammit, Lieutenant, are you going to contradict me at each turn or are you going to help me find a way to do something? If you want to spend your final days moping around auxiliary control, that's up to you. With or without you, I am going to find a way to help Spock."

Her pale, horsey face turned pink for a moment, and then, surprisingly, broke into an infectious smile. "Say the word, Captain."

Kirk grinned back. For a moment, he almost liked her.

"Welcome back, Spock."

The Vulcan's eyes slowly focused on McCoy as he sat up. "Where am I?"

"The academy," McCoy said. "Not too fast. I daresay you might find you still have a bit of a headache."

Spock reached a hand to his forehead in verification of McCoy's statement and blinked. "I was . . . home. . . ."

"Not anymore. I brought you back."

The Vulcan started. "Sarek—"

"He's here. I've got him set up in an isolation chamber. I've already run a few tests."

Spock sighed and swung his legs off the examination table. He began to stand.

"Take it easy." McCoy reached for the Vulcan's arm to support it, but Spock pulled it away.

He straightened his tunic. "I am quite all right, Doctor."

"Considering you damn near died of a skull fracture."

"As a result of my own clumsiness," Spock said ruefully. "I appreciate the fact that you and Dr. Lanter intervened on my behalf." He looked around the lab.

"She's in the isolation chamber," McCoy said quietly.

Spock turned his head sharply, but he did not ask McCoy to repeat what he had just said. For a moment, McCoy thought that Spock's legs would buckle, but the Vulcan did not sit, although he permitted himself to grasp the edge of the exam table with one hand.

"She wanted to confront Sarek herself," McCoy said. "I should never have let her go."

There was a long silence. "I am sure that there was nothing you could have done, Doctor. If you had gone with her, you would no doubt be affected as well. It is far better for both of us that you did not."

"I would like to believe that," McCoy said bitterly.

Spock stood straight once again, without the support of the table. "Then you brought the three of us here," he said, looking at McCoy with a curious expression.

"In a stolen skimmer. Believe me, it was no easy task, what with you coming to from time to time and commenting on my driving skills—"

Spock frowned. "I have no memory of doing so."

"People block out what they want to forget," McCoy said, trying to lighten things. "Let me tell you, it took me three trips to get all of you down here. It's a good thing this place is deserted these days." He rubbed his back. "I think I pulled a muscle."

"I am impressed, Dr. McCoy," Spock said quite sincerely.

"You ought to be. I think I've more than made up for the trouble I've caused."

"Most assuredly." Spock could not keep his eyes off the isolation chambers; finally, he walked stiffly to the other end of the lab. In one chamber, Anitra sat strapped in a chair, her head against the rest, her hair tangled and streaming down her shoulders. She was breathing deeply, her lips slightly parted. Sarek sat in the other chamber, regal even in repose. They looked very much as if they had never changed.

McCoy walked up and stood behind Spock. "I've got them both sedated. I had to keep them from coming to on the ride back."

"Of course," the Vulcan said distractedly. "It would be most . . . disconcerting if they were conscious." His eyes were fastened on Anitra's features, and for an instant his expression became so melancholic that McCoy decided he must have imagined it. Spock straightened his shoulders. "You said you had conducted some tests, Doctor?"

"Just a routine physical exam." McCoy glanced at the monitor above Anitra's head admiringly. "You were right about this place, Spock—what I wouldn't give for one like this back on the *Enterprise*." His tone became more sober. "General functions of all organs—normal—with one exception."

"Which is?"

"The neurotransmitters in the brain seem to have been altered slightly. I'll have to do some more testing before I can say exactly how."

Spock nodded. "It makes sense." He had been looking at Anitra the entire time, but now he turned to face McCoy. "You needed to bring only one subject back, Doctor. Anitra would have been the logical choice, since she is the most use to us. Yet you brought Sarek as well at great personal risk."

McCoy squirmed, uncomfortable himself with the real reason he could not leave Sarek behind. Not that he hadn't considered it, but after remembering what Anitra had told him, he had found it impossible. He cleared his throat. "It's a moot point, isn't it, Spock? I mean, Sarek is already here and there's no time to waste. The logical thing to do is to start testing."

"Why, Dr. McCoy," Spock said approvingly. "How eminently practical of you. Perhaps your stay on Vulcan has sharpened your capacity for logic."

"I sure as hell hope not," McCoy said under his breath.

McCoy had been napping, in spite of himself, on the exam table where he had performed surgery on Spock a few hours before. Something roused him from a heavy sleep—noise or light or a dream ending—and he pulled himself up, feeling every bit as drugged as the two in isolation.

Spock sat at the console facing the chambers. He

was frowning at the readout on the terminal in front of him. McCoy stumbled over, rubbing his eyes. "Anything new?"

The Vulcan swiveled the screen so that McCoy could read it. "An analysis of their blood chemistry. You were correct in noting it had changed. Certain elements that make up the neurotransmitters have indeed changed—their atomic weight is heavier, as though other particles had bonded with them to form isotopes."

McCoy sat down next to him. "And the neurotransmitters control the brain."

"Apparently, Dr. Lanter was correct in postulating that our demons exist on the subatomic level." Spock pulled the screen toward him again. "They chemically bond with the neurotransmitters of the host and thus control the host's actions."

"But neurotransmitters are stable compounds—you can't bond anything with them. And how in the hell can a subatomic particle think, let alone control someone's actions?"

Spock was unmoved by McCoy's vehemence. "You mentioned moot questions earlier, Doctor. The fact already exists—they have done so. And not only can these particles bond with the chemicals that control conscious actions, they also control the autonomic processes as well—pulse, breathing, digestion. . . ."

"That explains your mother seeming to be dead," McCoy said. "So how do we reverse this bonding process?"

Spock sighed. "There is no guarantee that it can be reversed. One way might be to find a compound which the particles prefer to bond with over neurotransmitters. In that case, our next step would be to test potential compounds."

"That could take forever. Isn't there any other way that the chemical bond could be broken?"

Spock hesitated. "Yes . . . there are ways, as you know, to split atoms. Such methods would, indeed, destroy the bond, and quite possibly the particles themselves." He looked directly into McCoy's bleary eyes. "They would also destroy the host. I would prefer to avoid that, but it might not be possible. If Dr. Lanter were able to help us . . ."

"The two of us can do it, Spock. With your brains—"

"Time is of the essence in our situation," Spock interrupted him. "And Dr. Lanter is a specialist in the area of particle physics. That is why Star Fleet assigned her to this. I have no doubt that she would have been able to help us find the solution far more rapidly."

"Another moot point," said McCoy. "Let's do the best we can without her. I'll get started testing compounds right away."

But before he could do anything, the monitor above Sarek's head beeped. McCoy hunched over the matching monitor on the console.

"What is it, Doctor?"

"I don't understand. I didn't give him that strong of a dose."

"Doctor," Spock said with a sharp note of exasperation.

"His life functions. They're growing weaker. Pulse

and breathing, brain activity—all are slowing, as if he were slipping into a coma."

Spock leaned over and read the monitor for himself. "Check Anitra's readings."

"She's all right," McCoy said. "Normal. But you'd better look at this, Spock. Sarek's brain chemistry is going haywire—the neurotransmitters are taking on a positive charge." He looked up at the Vulcan. "We've got to find a way to stop this soon."

"Or Sarek will die," Spock said softly.

Chapter Thirteen

McCoy ROSE FROM the console, stretched, and checked Sarek's monitor. The Vulcan was steadily growing weaker—it was a matter of a few hours now, if that. He turned to Spock, who was absorbed by the spectral analysis of 1-methodiobromidase.

"Any closer?"

Spock grunted assent. "This particular compound looks promising. It might quite possibly work."

"Great! Let's try it on a tissue sample."

Spock looked up from his terminal. "There is, however, one drawback."

McCoy looked at him questioningly.

"It is quite lethal to both humans and Vulcans."

"For God's sake, Spock, why didn't you say so? Then it's of no use to us." He bent over and routinely checked Anitra's monitor . . . and looked a second time.

"A metabolic slowdown," Spock said. It was not a question.

McCoy nodded, crushed. "She's a few hours behind Sarek." He turned to Spock. "We'd better start working on finding a nondeadly derivative."

"There is an alternative," Spock said slowly, steepling his hands. He began to intently study a distant point on the wall. "It will take an indefinite amount of time to find a safe derivative—days . . . perhaps weeks. Sarek and Anitra do not have that long." He took a breath and squared his shoulders. "I suggest we try the compound in its present form on Sarek."

"You'd poison your own father?!" McCoy was outraged. "What if we find the derivative an hour from now? Why are you in such a hurry?"

"Sarek doesn't have an hour." Spock's tone was even. "Or did you think that I didn't notice when you were checking the monitor?"

"You'd just as soon get it over with? Poison him now, is that it?"

Spock's voice deepened as he spoke through not-quite-clenched teeth. "He is going to die, Doctor. At least permit me to give his death some meaning."

McCoy closed his eyes. "Look . . . I'm sorry, Spock. I know this must be hard for you. But this can't be the solution. What will we do, spray Vulcan with poisonous gas? All of Vulcan? And what about your mother, and Jim, and everyone else on board the *Enterprise?* Are we going to let these damn particles win?"

"And if we cannot find a nonpoisonous derivative," Spock said, "are you, Doctor, willing to let them spread?"

"Glad you made it, sir," Tomson said most sincerely. The small filter she wore over her nose and mouth muffled her voice so that Kirk could scarcely recognize it.

He touched a hand to his face to make sure his own filter was in place; through the thick streams of gas, he could barely make out Tomson's form on the bridge. She'd already dragged the personnel from their posts, and they lay in an unceremonious heap by the turbo-lift.

"No more than I am," Kirk said. He held up the drifting device so that she could see it. "This is what caused all the trouble."

She leaned forward and squinted, trying to see. "It's hard to believe something that small . . . How soon will the engines be warmed up, Captain?"

"Thirty minutes. That ought to give us enough time, if we hustle." He turned toward the pile of sedated bodies and started pulling one into the still-open lift. "What about the other levels?"

Tomson made it over to Spock's station in two strides and snapped on the viewer. "Verified that all of C deck has been flooded. You shouldn't have any trouble, sir."

"Ready to flood D deck, corridors eight through eleven, F deck near auxiliary control. I'll give you the signal from the lift when I'm finished on C deck." He stopped what he was doing for an instant, and although she could not see his mouth behind the filter, she knew from his eyes that he beamed at her; she smiled back beneath her mask. "Good work, Lieutenant. It's not every security chief who can learn to do the work of an engineer so quickly."

Tomson blushed. "Engineering was my second choice, sir." She hesitated. "Are you sure I can't go with you?"

"Someone has to be on the bridge, Lieutenant. I

want the turbolift sealed off the second I'm finished. We can't risk someone figuring out what we're doing and beating me back here."

She nodded reluctantly, unable to let go of the feeling that she was somehow failing in her responsibilities by staying behind. She found it infinitely harder to handle the technical details and wait—but Kirk had insisted that she not risk herself, and she could not disobey a direct order. "Yes, sir," she said with a sigh. "I'll be standing by for your signal."

They crammed the last of the bodies onto the lift. Before it closed, Kirk gave her the thumbs-up signal.

She smiled and returned it.

McCoy had, for the time being at least, won the argument. Spock had continued rather grudgingly to search for a nonpoisonous derivative to test on Sarek, as had McCoy, but both of them knew Sarek was slipping away. McCoy slowly realized that, as much as he hated the thought, Spock was probably right. Even so, he could not knowingly permit the use of a poison on any patient—even one that would jump at the chance to brain him—especially when it was Spock's father or, God forbid, Anitra. And he was hoping that Spock would ultimately be unable to go through with it.

Within the chambers, Sarek and Anitra, pale and scarcely breathing, seemed something less than alive. Not dead, exactly; but they reminded McCoy of some pictures he had seen of museums where life-size images of real people were cast in wax. He felt the same eerie effect looking at Sarek and Anitra now—waxen effigies of what had once been real, living people. . . .

Up to now, Spock had scrupulously kept his eyes off the chambers and did not look when McCoy checked the monitors. It was extreme concentration on a task, McCoy decided, or an exercise in denial. He looked down at Anitra's monitor and wished he hadn't—her condition paralleled Sarek's. Soon she, too, would be in a coma, that gray nether world between life and death. It took him a while to get up the nerve to check Sarek's monitor; behind the glass, Sarek's lungs no longer seemed to expand with air. McCoy closed his eyes at the thought that Sarek had been dead these past few minutes, and he, McCoy, would have to tell Spock that he had not known. . . . McCoy opened his eyes and forced himself to look down.

He gasped audibly. Spock's perfect concentration was broken; he glanced over at McCoy, his expression unconvincingly calm, clearly expecting the worst.

"I don't understand it," McCoy said. His eyes were still glued to the monitor on the console. "By all rights, this man should be dead—"

Spock stood up.

"Come take a look, Spock." Without taking his eyes from the monitor, McCoy motioned him over and cracked a wide grin. "His life processes—they're getting stronger."

Spock walked over behind the doctor and read the monitor. Sarek was indeed stronger and no longer in a coma. Spock looked up; behind the glass, Sarek opened his eyes and frowned.

"Father," Spock whispered and walked to the edge of the chamber. He rested a hand lightly upon the glass.

All sound within the chamber was absorbed, but Sarek's lips moved clearly. "Spock?" they said.

Kirk had dumped the sedated officers off on C deck, and Tomson had flooded decks D and F. Then, once Kirk had removed the few unconscious personnel, she sealed off the corridors between the lift and the transporter on D and the lift and auxiliary control on F. With the ship in chaos, there were relatively few personnel on those levels, since these areas were generally frequented by those on duty.

Kirk called her from the lift. "That's it, Tomson. Go ahead and program the lift."

"And seal off the emergency shafts," she reminded him.

"There must be a commendation in there for you somewhere, Lieutenant."

Tomson bent over Spock's station (even in Spock's chair, she was too tall to read the viewer and had to hunch her shoulders) and programmed the lift. It would go now only to the transporter room, auxiliary control and the bridge. No matter how often others might try to signal it, it would ignore their requests, unless they somehow managed to get onto one of the three key floors.

And there was no way they could. Tomson settled back in Spock's chair, feeling quite pleased with herself.

Kirk came off the lift, his filter dangling from a strap around his neck; Tomson had already ventilated the bridge and removed her own mask.

He went directly to the navigational console, sat

down and manipulated a few controls. When he finally turned to speak to her, he was beaming. "On route to Vulcan. Congratulations, Lieutenant."

She walked over to him. "You mean we did it, sir?" She broke into a silly grin—so utterly silly that Kirk grabbed her arms and shook her enthusiastically, quite unaware of what he was doing. She grabbed his arms firmly and shook back.

"We did it!"

"We did it!"

It took them both a moment to realize that they were hugging; Tomson's ridiculous smile faded and she stiffened. Kirk, embarrassed, loosened his grip and took a step backward. But neither one of them could quite completely stop smiling.

Spock moved toward the isolation chamber, but McCoy put a hand on his arm. "Sorry, Spock, but I think we'd better test him out first."

Spock stopped. "I suppose you're right, Doctor." He stepped back while McCoy studied the monitor.

"His brain chemistry is back to normal," the doctor announced cheerfully. "He's all right."

Spock opened the door to the chamber and loosened Sarek's restraints. Sarek sat forward, still weak but growing in strength, and rubbed his wrists. "What place is this?"

"One of the medical laboratories at the academy," Spock said. "We brought you here."

"Have I been ill?"

Spock carefully avoided his father's gaze. "You . . . have not been yourself."

He led Sarek out of the chamber and sat him at one

of the chairs at the console; McCoy used the hand-held scanner and did a full physical on him, just to be sure.

"My wife and my brother," Sarek said. His face was still austere and stern, but now inspired respect rather than fear in McCoy. "Are they also here? Or are they in ShiKahr?"

Spock met McCoy's eyes for a moment before he made himself look directly into his father's. His voice was controlled, completely Vulcan, yet there was a strange softness in it that McCoy had not heard before.

"Mother is on the *Enterprise*. I do not know her status. Silek—" and he paused here, his voice becoming even softer, "—is dead."

Sarek sighed and directed his gaze toward Anitra; he seemed to be concentrating on her features. "How?" he asked.

McCoy watched Spock closely, unsure of what the Vulcan might say. "Murdered," Spock said, "by alien entities. He and Starnn both."

"Amanda," Sarek whispered. "Does she know?"

"She knows." Spock paused for a moment. "She is afflicted by them herself. The evil that destroyed Hydrilla has overtaken Vulcan. It spread from Starnn to you, and then Amanda; it has even taken over the crew of the *Enterprise*. They are entities that bond with the chemicals of the brain and thus control their host, causing him to commit violent, sadistic actions. The fact that you are now free of them means that there is hope that Amanda, and many on Vulcan, can also be free."

"How can they be freed?" Sarek asked. He was still watching Anitra and seemed to understand.

"I am not positive of the circumstances that brought about your freedom."

"Do you think it was the sedative I used?" McCoy asked.

Spock shook his head. "Negative—it was one of the first compounds we tested." He glanced at the chronometer on the console. "Do you have any idea, Doctor, when you first sedated them?"

"Not really," McCoy admitted. "I know it's been at least one standard solar day. Why would you ask?"

"You told me earlier that Anitra and Sarek spoke to you of 'feeding,'" Spock said slowly. "Apparently, they indicated that they regularly needed to feed off another's terror, or find a new host. They used the plural pronoun 'we.' It might be that the entities kept multiplying and either had to be fed or transferred to another host. If the energy supply were cut off—"

"That would explain the odd change in Sarek's brain chemicals," McCoy said excitedly. "Don't you realize what this means? We've beaten the damn things!"

Spock seemed unmoved. "Not necessarily, Doctor. Unless you have a simple suggestion for isolating all those on Vulcan."

Sarek emerged suddenly from his reverie. "Sedation was obviously quite effective. If the host was incapacitated, it would keep them from spreading or feeding, would it not?"

"Yes," said Spock. "But logistically, how do we sedate an entire planet for more than a solar day?"

"I'm afraid you have a point there," said McCoy.

"Once an appropriately long-lasting sedative is found," Sarek responded, "it might conceivably be introduced into the water supply—"

"But exposure to the sedative would then vary, depending on the amount of water drunk. And there might be those who would not drink from the main reserves at all. Then there exists the problem of getting a sufficient quantity of the sedative into all of the main reserves."

"Perhaps a gaseous form," Sarek mused.

"Those locked inside would not be affected," said Spock.

"Only humans, most likely," Sarek pointed out. "Vulcans usually ventilate their buildings using air from outside. And as for those who might be sealed inside, you indicated yourself that they must go in search of new victims on a regular basis."

"It might be possible. We would need a gas which has a long-lasting, sedative effect, works on humans and Vulcans and stays in the atmosphere for at least several hours." Spock ticked them off on his fingers. "Now the only problems that exist are to isolate such a gas, manufacture sufficient quantities of it and find a way to disperse it into Vulcan's atmosphere."

"Simple," McCoy said ironically.

"The box." There was an urgent note in Sarek's voice. "There are several of them at the academy and one at the house. My last memory is that of looking into the open box. . . ."

"It would be interesting to study one," Spock suggested.

"No. That is how the Hydrillan expedition was first affected. Then they brought the boxes with them in order to spread it further."

"Interesting," Spock mused. "Then the box serves to house the particles. But why would such constructs be required if they spread so easily from host to host?"

"Hydrilla has been dead some twenty thousand years, and yet the particles survived. Perhaps they had hosts design the container for just such an occurrence."

"It is an effective means of storage," Spock replied, "but the Hydrillans were not even capable of space flight beyond their own solar system. How could they have designed such a sophisticated device?"

Sarek paused for a moment. "They could not. But it might have been designed earlier by a more technologically advanced culture, the one that originally spread the particles to Hydrilla—"

McCoy interrupted. "It hardly matters. What we need to do is get rid of the things."

Spock frowned at him. "If their contents have not already been exhausted."

"A very likely possibility," Sarek said.

"I'm not so sure it can be repaired," Tomson said. She sat cross-legged on the deck. The panel beneath the communications board had been pulled away, and she gazed up uncertainly into a maze of microcircuitry. She leaned back and, without having to stand up, could just see over the edge enough to access the computer. Even with the computer's help, the condition in which Anitra had left communications was intimidating.

"It can be repaired," Kirk said firmly from the navigational console. "We don't have a choice. We're entering orbit now."

"Already?" Tomson asked in dismay. She turned

around to see the red giant spinning leisurely in its orbit, then hastened back to her work on the board; she was nowhere near patching external communications together.

Kirk's answer was interrupted by a thunderous roar. The ship pitched to the left and sent Tomson rolling along the deck with a yelp. She stopped directly in front of the turbolift; the doors opened in response, waiting. Kirk held onto the navigational console and waited for the ship to slowly right itself.

"What the—" Tomson said.

Kirk already had the deflectors up. "We've been fired on. Activate starboard view screen, Lieutenant."

Tomson raised herself and studied Uhura's console helplessly. "On this panel, sir?"

"To your left, Lieutenant," he barked.

Tomson found it; the screen filled with the image of a sleekly designed starship.

Kirk swore under his breath. "That looks like one of ours. See if you can raise—" he began, then corrected himself. "Magnify that image."

Tomson forced herself to react faster than the last time. She chose a button on the panel; the image shimmered and enlarged.

"The *Surak*," Kirk said. "What the hell is a Federation starship full of Vulcans doing firing on us?"

Tomson was miserable. "I'm sorry, sir—it's my fault we can't contact them."

"I don't need apologies, Lieutenant. I need a damage report—you can get that from the main terminal." He was readying the photon torpedoes as another blast shook the bridge.

"No casualties reported—" Tomson began.

"I wouldn't have expected them to," he said tautly. "What about the ship?"

"Minor structural damage to the jettison pods. Nothing significant, sir."

"I never thought I'd be doing this." Kirk fired the photon torpedoes in a barrage of three.

The *Surak* backed off.

"Looks like you hit them, sir," Tomson said excitedly.

"Looks like it." Kirk sighed. "Even after that board is fixed, Tomson, I want to maintain radio silence. Don't respond to anyone—not even Vulcan Space Central. I'm not so sure we're going to get a warm reception."

Anitra smiled faintly in response to the broad grin on McCoy's face; slowly, her expression faded to one of uncertainty. "Sarek," she said, frowning. She leaned forward in her chair and looked out of the chamber; when she saw him on the other side of the glass, she nearly bolted. "Oh, my God . . ."

McCoy held her back with a reassuring arm on her shoulder. "It's all right. He's all right now."

"Spock—is he—"

"He's fine. You can't hurt someone with a head as thick as his."

She smiled again weakly. "Don't let him hear you say that. We're in the lab again, aren't we? How'd we get here?"

"I brought you."

She closed her eyes. "I'm so sorry. I was so certain I could handle Sarek without any problem. . . . It must have been horrible for you."

"The worst part was bringing Spock back to consciousness."

She laughed. "If Sarek is all right, you must have found the answer. That's wonderful! Tell me everything."

"It seems," said McCoy, "that these . . . critters multiply so rapidly that they have to feed, or find a new host—or die. That's what happened to them when we kept you and Sarek isolated for a day." He nodded at Spock and Sarek. The two sat at the console, calmly arguing about something—hopefully, the best means of implementing the plan. McCoy cleared his throat. "Maybe you two gentlemen should consult Dr. Lanter before you make any definite decisions."

Sarek nodded politely, as if to a somewhat unfamiliar acquaintance. There was uncertain recognition on his face, as if he remembered and yet could not remember their most recent encounter.

"Dr. Lanter," Spock said with a formality that was belied by the brightness in his eyes, "I am glad to see you are feeling like yourself once again."

"I'm glad, too," she said. "What exactly are you two discussing?"

Spock explained it to her. "We've already located the sedative we need in the computer's medical index. It ought to be possible to manufacture a sufficient quantity here. However, we were discussing the problem of administering the drug to the general population."

"Gaseous form would be the most logical," Anitra said.

"We are agreed on that."

"Good," she said. "Then we'd need some station-

235

ery antigravity buoys set up in the lower atmosphere—something time delayed or remote controlled. A transporter would be the best thing for setting them in place, but since we haven't got one, we could probably use a skimmer to position them. We wouldn't need to go that high up."

"And God knows you're already an expert at stealing skimmers," McCoy retorted, but he was ignored.

Spock grunted. "The physics lab might contain some of what you'd need for the buoys."

"Great," she said. "Let's get working."

There was a sudden loud noise that made McCoy jump—a sound at once familiar and frightening. It was coming from Spock's communicator on the console. Spock froze.

"Don't answer it," McCoy told him. "It's some kind of trick."

"If they've found the communicators," Spock said, "they've found us. It hardly makes any difference whether I answer or not. Besides, it could be Lieutenant Uhura."

McCoy looked searchingly at Anitra. "Don't look at me," she said, waving him away. "I told you, I'm no good at long distance. I have no idea who it is."

"Maybe if we don't answer it," said McCoy, "they'll think we're not here."

Spock spoke as patiently as if he were explaining something to a dim-witted child. "Doctor, they can easily scan the area and ascertain exactly who is here. They have probably already done so. If they were going to attack us, they would gain no advantage by contacting us first." He picked up the communicator and snapped it open. "Spock here."

"Spock! You're all right!"

"Is this the captain?" Spock asked. There was more than a little chill in his voice.

"I know what you're thinking, Spock, but Uhura knocked me over the head and stuffed me into a closet. I know it sounds crazy, but when I came to—"

"Actually, Captain, it makes an enormous amount of sense," Spock said gratefully.

"It's Jim, isn't it?" McCoy exulted. "Well, I'll be damned. I should have known he'd get that ship up and running."

"Bones, is that you?" Kirk asked.

Spock handed the communicator to McCoy. "Guess what, Jim? We've got a little sedative down here that's guaranteed to drive the devil right out of a body—"

Spock took the communicator back. "What the doctor is trying to say, Captain, is that sedation works as well as isolation."

"Are you sure about that, Spock? We've already gassed most of the crew and it hasn't seemed to have any effect—"

"It would not, unless they were sedated for the proper amount of time. An extended period of isolation is required. This sedative has an especially long-lasting effect, with, hopefully, the same outcome. It ought to work."

"You're going to single-handedly gas all of Vulcan?"

Spock paused. "I have the help of three others, sir."

"You know what I mean."

"Basically, yes."

"Then I'm volunteering the *Enterprise* as a test site. I've got four hundred very unpleasant crew members

237

sealed off on this ship. Why not try it on a small scale first?"

Spock looked at McCoy and Anitra, who both nodded. "Captain, is your transporter functioning and can you get to it safely?"

"Yes."

"We'll be setting aside some canisters of gas for you to beam up, sir. It'll take some time, but we'll notify you when they're ready." He paused. "I would be most interested in hearing the results."

Chapter Fourteen

TOMSON SAT AT Uhura's station, grinning her huge, lopsided smile. "The calls, Captain. They're coming in from all over the ship. They want to know what's going on."

Kirk grinned back. "What do you think we ought to tell them, Lieutenant?"

"How about—we'll explain everything to them later."

"Sounds good to me." Kirk swiveled in his command chair to face her. "Make a shipwide announcement, Tomson. Tell all members of the bridge crew they're now considered late reporting for duty and it's twenty demerits if they don't get up here on the double."

Tomson chuckled. "Aye, sir."

She made the announcement and watched as the lights on the board flashed dizzyingly in response. She closed her eyes. "I was wondering, sir—" She hesitated.

Kirk raised his eyebrows quizzically.

"There's someone I'd like to check on personally—

when the bridge crew gets here, that is—if it's all right."

Kirk looked around the bridge. "I think I can hold down the fort by myself until everyone gets here." He smiled. "You go on ahead."

Tomson blushed at the unexpected kindness. "Thank you, sir."

She left the bridge with what seemed to Kirk like an alarming amount of haste. He shook his head in surprise. It was hard for him to imagine anyone on board who would be that important to the cold-hearted Tomson—but then, one never knew. He had already had a glimpse of what lay under all that ice. . . .

In the turbolift, Tomson fingered the phaser on her belt with trembling hands. She had been waiting for this for a long time; when he had called in and given his location, she could hardly believe her luck. Now, if she could only get him alone, for just a moment, no one would be the wiser. They would simply assume it was part of the carnage that had gone on before. . . .

The lift deposited her on D deck, junior officers' quarters. She passed a couple of crewmen in the corridor and took care to look as dazed and lost as they did. In their present state, they would never notice another crew member wandering around the hall.

She had not been able to forget exactly where Stryker's quarters were. The door opened at the first buzz.

Stryker looked quite honestly surprised—and hardly military—he had at least a week's growth of beard. His pale eyes were red-rimmed, as though he hadn't slept in at least as long. "Lieutenant! Maybe you can tell me what's going on."

"Maybe I can," she said. Her hand shook as she raised the phaser.

"Hey, wait a minute!" Stryker's colorless eyes darkened with fear. "What in hell is this all about?"

"You don't remember." Tomson's voice was as listless as a sleepwalker's.

"Remember what?"

"Moh's dead."

Stryker's face twisted. "Al-B? Dead?"

"You killed him."

"You're crazy! I don't know anything about it. I didn't even know he was dead!" He took a step closer to a dresser, but Tomson gestured with the phaser in such a way as to let him know that if he took another step, he would not live long enough for his foot to strike the ground.

"You don't know because you don't remember," she said in a flat, mechanical voice. "But you killed him."

The pain on Stryker's face was so sharp that she felt it, as keenly as she had felt it when she had first seen al-B dead. She had to look away.

Surprisingly, he did not take advantage of her inattention. Instead, he leaned against the wall and crumpled to the ground, weeping. "Moh's dead . . . God, if it's really true, then go ahead and shoot me."

She had prepared herself for such a reaction from him . . . but she had not prepared herself for her own. Sobbing, she went over and put her arms around him.

*   *   *

Uhura awoke slowly, feeling pleasantly rested, and began to stretch. It seemed that she'd been sleeping too long in the same position. It was then that she noticed two things: one, that she was in a strange room with no memory of how she had gotten there, and two, that she was in Sulu's arms. She gasped so loudly at the latter revelation that the helmsman, whose nose was at most two inches from her own, opened his left eye and gasped back.

They extricated themselves from a most curious embrace—a jumble of arms and legs—murmuring vague apologies all the while. Uhura was glad her complexion was too dark to show the blood rushing to her face, but Sulu was not as fortunate.

"What—" he began, then became confused about which question should most appropriately be asked first, and started again. "Where are we?"

Uhura frowned. There was a void in her memory, as though someone had neatly plucked out all recall of the most recent events. She concentrated on the last thing she remembered happening—and, realizing that Sulu was the enemy, made a quick scramble for the small dagger that lay only a few feet away on the floor. She grimaced sickly as she picked it up—it had blood on it—but recovered quickly, and, still on her knees, brandished it at Sulu. He had watched, sitting quietly on the floor, too amazed to react. He looked at the dagger and then, on some instinct, down at his chest. He had been sliced diagonally across his torso, not deeply enough to cause any real damage, but enough to cut through the fabric of his tunic and stain it with blood.

"Hey," he said, his dark eyes wide with a mixture of

anger and confusion, "ease up, Uhura. Just what do you think you're gonna do with that thing?"

"Don't come near me," Uhura threatened.

"Okay, I won't," Sulu said. He was still too indignant to be frightened. "Why'd you go and cut me like this?"

Uhura hesitated and sat back on her haunches. "I honestly don't know. I just remember I had this hidden on me and I think . . . we were trying to kill each other."

"Kill each other!" Sulu scoffed, but then he eyed his tunic. "Maybe we were," he said in a voice full of wonder, "but I still don't understand."

Tomson's voice came through the intercom, and they sat listening to it.

"What's she doing up there?" Uhura demanded haughtily.

"I don't see you up on the bridge," Sulu countered. "Be quiet and listen."

When the message finished, Sulu got to his feet. "I still don't understand what's going on."

"I understand part of it," Uhura said. "I can explain it to you on our way up to the bridge."

"Last one there's a—" Sulu said and impacted with the door. "What the—"

"We're locked in." Uhura was indignant. "Call the bridge and find out what's going on."

Scott found himself stretched out in the corridor near engineering. He yawned and rose stiffly, put a hand to his mouth, and noticed there was a phaser in it, fully charged and set to kill. He clicked his tongue and changed it to the lowest setting. When he looked up, he saw the bulkhead where it came to a corner in front of him; it was scorched, having very nearly been blown away.

"What the devil—" He walked around the corner and saw Chekhov on the other side, struggling to get to his feet.

"Mr. Scott," the navigator said. "I seem to have been knocked unconscious—"

"Ye're not the only one, laddie." Scott hoisted him to his feet. "I was lyin' just on the other side there."

Chekhov hissed, pointing. "The bulkhead, sir, look!" On his side, the outer wall had been blown away, exposing the minute circuitry beneath. "We had better call security. Who would do such a thing?"

Without answering, Scott bent down and retrieved the phaser near Chekhov's feet. It, too, was set to kill. Scott lowered the setting, but not without showing it to Chekhov first.

"Apparently, laddie, we did."

Amanda was remembering with perfect clarity; she had sat outside the door of the study, imagining what she would say to Sarek. She closed her eyes and pictured herself going inside; Sarek would be sitting at the computer terminal, and when she entered, he would gaze up calmly at her. And then she would do what she had never done before—rage and weep and flail her arms at him, spit venom at him, and make cruel and hurtful remarks about the things he had done to Spock, to her, all the things not forgotten over the years. She would say that she had raised a child who could not love her, and that it had broken her heart. She would say that he had scarred the boy, made him be ashamed to be what he was. She would say that life on Vulcan was unbearable, that it had been a horrible mistake to bring her here. . . .

And when she could think of nothing more to hurt him with, she would stand, trembling, with tears on her face. And Sarek would sit, unmoving and unmoved, his impassive eyes fixed on her, and he would say nothing.

And in her dream she saw what had really happened. She opened her eyes and saw that the door to Sarek's study was still closed. Inside, it was dark, except for the glow emanating from the terminal. Sarek gazed up and waited for her to speak. She rarely interrupted him while he was working.

She clasped her hands in front of her, and in a carefully measured voice said, "I must talk to you about Spock."

He knew, of course, that she was angry; he always knew what she was feeling, no matter how hard she tried to hide it from him. "Then speak," he said. He sounded tired, although his face did not show it.

"I have always tried to do as you have asked," she said, struggling to keep her voice steady, "and I have never asked much of you. But I cannot—" She broke off and lowered her head. Sarek waited quietly. "—I cannot choose between the two of you. I can't give one of you up. Please don't ask me to make that kind of choice."

Sarek snapped the terminal off and sat quietly in his chair for some time; Amanda could no longer see his expression. At last he rose and moved toward her. She still could not see his face, but even in the darkness she could see that he held out his hand.

"Sarek."

She woke herself up saying the name aloud. She was sitting up on a bed in a room that she did not recognize. Something had happened to her, something that she could not remember . . . she closed her eyes and tried to remember.

Sarek. She felt a sickening wave of terror; he had changed, had become something else . . . something horrible. With grief and revulsion, she remembered Silek.

But where was she now? There was something familiar about the place, as though she had been here before, perhaps with Sarek. . . .

The starship. She put her feet on the floor and went to find Spock.

"It worked!"

Spock raised both eyebrows at the shout that emanated from his communicator. Next to him, Anitra and McCoy grinned.

"Are you quite sure, Captain?"

"The bridge crew is straggling in, making their apologies. They all seem to be their affable selves again." Kirk exchanged smiles with Uhura and Sulu, both at their stations. "What can we do to help you at this end?"

"The buoys will be ready soon, Captain. When you have someone manning the transporter room, we'll send them up and then feed you the coordinates for their placement in the atmosphere."

"Let me know when you're ready. Oh, and Mr. Spock . . ."

"Captain?"

"I have someone here who will be beaming down shortly." He smiled over at Amanda.

The city began falling asleep. On the streets, a few souls dropped in their tracks and slept where they fell. In the air above them, passengers in skimmers slumped over their control panels and were gently shepherded by the computer to their pre-programmed destinations. They never disembarked. The thin, white cloud descended and found its way into homes, buildings, even the caverns of Gol, where T'Sai and her followers slept. It filled the halls of the empty academy—except for the one room which had been sealed with lead walls. People fighting, strangling, killing each other, fell to the ground together, locked in gruesome embraces.

The planet Vulcan slept, and the evil faded.

EPILOGUE

"I think I need to talk to you," Anitra said. She stood hesitantly in the doorway of McCoy's quarters.

"Come in, my dear." McCoy smiled warmly. "Can I get you something to drink?"

"Absolutely," she said before he'd even had a chance to finish the question. "I assume it'll be sour mash."

"Bourbon. Sour mash is mighty hard to find out here."

"It'll do." She stood and looked around, obviously uncomfortable, as he poured the drinks. Her eyes were large and bright.

He turned away from the cabinets and gave her one of the glasses he was holding. "Don't tell me. Let me guess. It has something to do with your leaving the service."

Her jaw dropped. "How'd you know?"

"Sit down, Anitra, and relax."

She took a seat and he sat across from her behind the desk and held up his glass in a toast. "To your leaving the service."

She raised her drink but did not smile. "You sound almost happy about it."

"Quite the contrary. I am heartbroken. But I want what's best for you." He said it softly so that she would understand he was serious, then took a swallow of the whiskey.

"Funny, I feel exactly the same way." She drank and leaned forward with a conspiratorial air. "You wanted to know about the ulcer. Now that I'm leaving, I can say that it had something to do with the fact that I wasn't cut out for intelligence work."

"I thought it was just the one 'project'—"

She shook her head. "They were always after me to get involved in more projects for them. It was beginning to get very political—" She took a huge gulp of her drink. "I don't feel guilty. I've done my duty—the galaxy is once again safe for the Federation's particular brand of democracy, so I told them where to put their projects and resigned my commission."

"Good for you," McCoy said approvingly. "And I understand that the Vulcans are once again their logical selves."

"Yes, but the toll on the population was great. Spock told me they found two of the boxes with the contents still intact."

"My God! What did they do with them?"

"You know the Vulcans. They're on display at the academy museum."

McCoy stiffened. "Are they insane? What if one of those damn things decides to open?"

Anitra shrugged and sipped her drink calmly. "Nothing will happen. They've got them shrouded behind a dozen force fields."

"Well . . ." McCoy said grudgingly, "I still think they're asking for trouble."

"If they are, you know what to do, Doctor."

He smiled at that, but it faded quickly. "Where will you go?"

"Back home, I think. I'd like to do private research, maybe with my dad."

"We're all really going to miss you."

"Promise me something," she said, her violet eyes large with sorrow.

"Anything," McCoy said gently, suddenly touched.

"Promise me you won't let them take the microphone out of the captain's shower again. I went to *so* much trouble this last time."

"Why you—" McCoy said.

She grinned, an imp once again.

Beyond the outskirts of ShiKahr lay the small shrine that housed the city's dead. There were no bodies there, merely polished black markers, each inscribed with two names: the name by which the deceased was known to all written in modern Vulcan, and the family name in ancient script. Recently, the number of new markers had increased startlingly.

Spock knelt forward and brushed the sand away from two of the markers. T'Ylle and Silek were not physically here; the sand was too soft and shifting for burial. Their bodies had been cremated, and Sarek, as the closest living relative, had scattered the ashes on the desert wind. They were a part of the roaming desert tide now, part of the sand that polished the markers until they glistened in the sun.

Spock touched the markers of the aunt and uncle he

had never seen alive. To both of them, the planet owed its thanks, and they would never know. But the family would remember.

After a time, he rose and headed slowly toward the city. Behind him, the wind stirred, uncovering a small object left by a mourner on Silek's grave.

Encased in heavy crystal, forever safe from the ravages of wind and sand, was a small, perfect yellow rose.